TERRAPIN

NORDIC AIRRE, BOOK ONE

To: Jenna

Love,
AC Trayer

Cover by Sarah Hansen www.okaycreations.com

Interior design and formatting by

www.emtippettsbookdesigns.com

TERRAPIN

NORDIC AIRRE, BOOK ONE

BY

A.C. TROYER

For Jeff, MaKenzi, and Kamryn.

"The greater the difficulty, the more glory in surmounting it. Skillful pilots gain their reputation from storms and tempests."

- Epictetus

ONE

My screaming stopped. Nightmares stole my sleep, and sweat drenched my skin. *Again.* I sat up, gasping for air. Silence.

Suffocating silence.

I shoved the quilt back and swung my legs over the edge of the bed, wiping shaky hands down my damp face. I closed my eyes for a moment and pulled in a deep breath. It was a hell of a way to wake up, but I was used to it. Except this time, it was different...darker and more violent somehow.

It was in the quiet moments after my nightmares that got me when I was alone in the dark and it was impossible to pretend I had a grip on my past, on the things I could never change or erase from my memory. A few minutes later, when I couldn't get the image out of my mind, I tried to remind myself the walls weren't caving in on me and the boys weight no longer trapped me beneath him. I released a frustrated sigh and rubbed a hand across my chest, snagging the chain around my neck between my fingers, nearly ripping it off.

I clasped the antique locket dangling from the necklace and brushed the cool metal between my fingers then opened it. The place where a picture should be was nothing more than a smooth stone with brown, green and hints of red. The locket was a departing gift from my mother—the woman who gave birth to me, then abandoned me. Perhaps the small token was her way of making up for abandoning me—tossing me into a home for misfits, the unwanted.

Try as I might, I couldn't lie to myself, though. She didn't want me. I wondered if a time would come when I would forget the inconvenient building with small windows, low rooms, dark staircases and the sadistic boy that haunted my dreams.

My gaze drifted to the alarm clock beside my bed.

"I've got to get out of here," I whispered to myself.

I hurried from my bed and quietly got dressed in my riding leathers and buckled the straps on my boots. Not wanting to lose the keepsake, I unclasped the chain and placed it on my tidy dresser. Like clockwork. Routine.

Casper's light snores echoed through the hall of our tiny apartment. My roommate had always been the careful one, the rule follower. The one who'd seen me slip in and out during curfew, never saying a word or asked questions. She kept my little secret. Therefore, I trusted her. I paused for a moment, then pulled back her door a sliver, and peered in. The moonlight leaked into the small bedroom, providing enough illumination to see her face.

Casper stirred and said softly, "You're awake?" I could hear the disappointment in her voice.

"I couldn't sleep," I said, watching her push up on her elbows. "I'm sorry I woke you up."

"Be careful. Don't get caught, Jinx," she said, and meant it. She knew the fine line I walked, but the blunt reminder grated my nerves. Recently, two Nordic P.I.T.'s (Pilots in Training) went missing. It was as if the world beneath their feet opened up and swallowed them whole, disappearing without a trace. Since then, everyone was on edge. Commander DeMarco implicated stricter rules and policies on his people, enforcing harsher punishments, and our little freedoms seemed to shrivel before our eyes. Not that I ever had any. Transferred from the orphanage to the military, I was Nordic's property indefinitely.

I looked her in the eyes, made myself smile although I wanted to scream. "I'll see you at the base," I replied, then left, slipping through the back sliding glass doors to the courtyard.

Sticking to the shadows, I pushed away from the safety of the wall, slinking to my motorcycle beneath the rusted carport. Sweat pooled beneath the leather riding gloves—anxiety and restlessness seeped into my bones. I slapped down the onyx shield of my helmet, started the engine, and then I flipped the head beams off so no one would see me. I gripped the handlebars like a life preserver, then twisted the throttle and took off.

Light poles emitted pools of warped light along the crumbling deserted street, not a single Night Watch or drone within sight. Airborne particles kicked up from a gust of wind, and a shadow fluttered between the Airre Guards housing structures.

I glanced over my shoulder, but nothing was there. *Maybe I should turn around.* Instead, I ordered my conscience to quit its bitching. Every treasured minute was worth the colossal risk I took, the veiled lookout on the mountainside calmed me. I clung to the handlebars, straightened and shook off my anxiety as the wheels spun against the pavement.

Every morning I told myself *one more time, one more time and I'll stop*, but that slice of independence pie rapidly became a sugary addiction I couldn't shake.

With caution, I took my time covering the uninhabited twelve miles on the empty road to my secret spot on the mountain, Sender's Rock. Easing the throttle, I steered the bike onto a dirt trail lined by thick rows of towering trees and snarling branches. The winding path thinned out, the sky opened up to a clearing where light bloomed and stars faded. Pulling back on the brakes a mere inch from a treacherous drop, I felt a sudden rush of excitement. I smiled behind the visor and let a current of air escape my mouth. My heart pounded against my ribs, and my unease subsided with every breath.

Nordic Airre gleamed amber below—nestled like a mounted gem between four prongs of emerald hills. Though temporary, I was free. I waved away the dust, dropped the kickstand and pulled off my helmet.

"So beautiful." A man's voice bit through the blackness.

Icy fear ran through me, eradicating my blissful freedom. I whirled around. A gasp of horror caught in my throat.

Within seconds, I recognized the leather-covered body leisurely leaning against a tree trunk. Ghost—the jet pilot every girl fawned over and he knew it. Sleek but silent, his chocolate eyes danced up and down my body, assessing me like a nifty new toy he couldn't wait to get his hands on. A cocky smirk pulled at the corner of his perfect, pouty lips.

I narrowed my eyes, noticing the red band circling his left bicep—the Commander's Seal. *No.*

The insignia Ghost wore gave him the privilege to police, capture or detain suspicious people. It sent fear into my heart. How could such a small strip of fabric possess so much power? Imprisoned by fear and the illusion of safety, the urge to run consumed me.

He pushed away from the tree and strode forward, never dropping his inquisitive eyes from mine. I stirred under his gaze, fidgeting with the helmet still in my grasp. Metal buckles clinked against his black riding boots.

"What did you just say?" I managed to say evenly, though the thought of him dragging me to the cells twisted my stomach into a tangled web of knots. I knew damn well, what he said. Considering the source, I also knew what his seductive half-mooned smile meant.

He gave me a lazy grin. "It's a cruel beauty, isn't it?"

The sun peaked over the horizon highlighting his bronze skin and strong jaw. Flecks of gold tamed the depth of his muddy eyes. He averted his eyes and kicked out his chin, directing his focus over my shoulder.

I followed his gaze, where a pallet of orange and yellow

ignited, drowning out the indigo sky. Nordic *was* the land of cruel beauty, where distance concealed cracked foundations and uniformity cloaked misfortunes. I swallowed a lump of raw emotion, remembering why I disobeyed curfew in the first place.

A tingling sensation assaulted me as Ghost's body drew near. A heady mixture of leather, clove and something earthy cloaked me.

"I have to go," I lied, hoping he would pull away and put distance between us. Never would I let him know how he affected me, or that the red cloth circling his arm threw me into a state of panic. Casper's warning rang in my ears. *Be Careful.* "I'm supposed to report in at zero eight-hundred."

I began to place my helmet back on when his hand clutched my wrist, stopping me. Every muscle in my body tensed. "Don't touch me." I assumed he would withdraw his hand immediately, but he held his ground and took an intimidating step closer.

"Have you lost your damn mind? What's wrong with you!" His demeanor changed, and he held my glare. "Don't you realize how stupid and dangerous it is for you to be out here alone?"

"Are you saying I should write my last will and testament" Sarcasm dripped in my voice.

Inwardly I chided myself. If he turned me in, or the Watch caught me prowling around during curfew … A shiver danced down my spine. Not all prisons were surrounded by iron bars; ours were invisible barriers of fear and violent repercussions.

"I'm saying you'd be suspended in a heartbeat. And your wings—" He ran a hand through his short brown hair and then pinched the bridge of his nose. He bent forward, staring at me with a worried expression. "It's no secret how good you are up there."

He lifted a pointed finger to the cloudy sky.

"Everyone sees it. I see it. One poor choice…that's all it takes, just one." He released my arm and calmly gave me room. "And it's gone. Worse yet, whoever abducted those young soldiers wouldn't second guess taking a pretty girl. You're smarter than that, Jinx."

"You think I don't know that?" Why would my comrade care what happened to me when this was the perfect opportunity to knock me out of my ranking for good?

Anyone who wore the band was exempt from the curfew law, allowing passage to and from any location within the country, but primarily for work related orders. I knew damn well he was here on his own volition. And I wanted to know why.

Ghost crossed his arms. "Where's your communicator?"

"Why not cut the crap and tell me why you're really here Ghost. I find it quite odd you managed to be in this exact location when no one knows about it but me. Are you following me?"

"You're right. Maybe I am. But for a few good reasons. Advisor Turner wants our squadron to report at zero seven-thirty." His body shifted, then paused to consider his answer, his expression calm and composed. "Our flights are going out early today. The message went out twenty minutes ago, and I was wondering why you were going the wrong way?"

My stupid communicator didn't go off again. My hand

patted along my waistline, searching for my communicator and came out empty-handed. I remembered setting it down while getting dressed. Distracted by thoughts, by my earlier nightmare I never picked it up. I was confused and shaken, more than I ever had been. It felt too real. And in my confusion, I'd made a dire mistake.

"Shit."

One poor choice—that's all it takes—just one. And it's gone. Had Ghost not followed me, I wouldn't have known about the commander's message.

He started to say something, but I cut him off and said, "I have to go!"

I could still make it to the apartment to grab my device and check in at headquarters on time if I hurried. I buckled the chinstrap and mounted my bike. The engine started up, and I put it into gear.

"One more infraction and I'm ground-bound," I shouted before twisting the throttle and shooting forward. It was true. After my first warning, Advisor Turner threatened to take away my flying privileges, keeping my feet planted on the ground.

I could feel the full weight of Ghost's undivided attention on me as I took off. As I sped down the road, I had to wonder if he'd ever followed me before. He always put himself first whether in class or training. Why look out for me now?

I rolled up along the curb outside my apartment and cut the engine. The squadron was already gone, leaving the Airre Guard apartments eerily quiet. Beside the front door, I placed my thumb over the security identification scanner, tapping my foot eagerly. The lock clicked and I pushed my way inside, not bothering to take my boots off. Gray industrial-grade carpet lined the hall throughout the military-issued, two-bedroom apartment. It was plain but, for the last three years, Casper and I called it home.

As I turned the corner and opened my bedroom door, a blast of air hit me. The tan curtains billowed as another blast of chilled air rushed through the opened window. I held still and silent. I didn't remember leaving the window open.

"Casper?" I called out wearily. "Someone here?"

No one answered, but it did little to ease the feeling that someone had been in my room. I rushed to close and lock the window. Then grabbing my communication device, I rushed from the room and through the house. I couldn't ignore the prickling sensation on the back of my neck as I left the apartment in a hurry.

Jogging to my motorcycle, I was on the road and headed toward the main gate in no time. The airfield loomed ahead. As usual, there were guards stationed outside. They had guns strapped around their chest and armed with deadly determination. Most days the base felt like a prison with its' towering chain-link fence with spiraling barbed wire encasing the top. In a way, it was a constant reminder of my time in the orphanage, surrounded by an iron choker, and always under a watchful eye.

A square metal box jutted out from the side of the brick and mortar guard station. Rolling up to it, I withdrew my hand from its leather glove, and placed my palm atop the square glass fixture. A red light scanned over my palm, then turned a flashing green. "Access Approved" blinked across the monitor screen situated above the scanner.

Ghost's sleek black bike thundered up behind me. He had an uncanny ability to fade into the background or appear out of nowhere when least expected. His riding suit emphasized his toned physique, stretching across the length of his shoulders and down his biceps.

My left leg bounced with anticipation. The gates slowly retracted and my bike shot forward, leaving Ghost in a cloud of smoking rubber. I couldn't help but smile in smug satisfaction.

The all-too-familiar sound of a throaty A-80 reverberated through the air as the sleek gunmetal beast took flight. Raging fumes blasted from the engines powerful thrust, pushing the jet higher in altitude. Ghost didn't lie to me. Another group lined up on the runway for takeoff.

I quickly pulled into the pilot parking deck. Cutting the engine, I pulled my helmet off and strapped it to my bike. I threw my riding gloves in the side compartment and ran my fingers through my hair. A thick brown wave streaked with purple dye fell over my shoulder. Binding it in a sloppy bun, I rushed toward the Operations Bay. I hiked up my backpack higher onto my shoulders and pulled the comm from my waistline.

A loud whistle startled me, causing my hands to fumble the comm.

"Hey, Jinx…looking good!" Someone catcalled.

A chorus of whistles followed the remarks. A rowdy group

of P.I.T. ogled me as I rushed by. They wore the traditional Cadet uniforms. Gray and red canvas jacket emblazoned with a harbinger seal of wings embossed in metal—declaring their ranking for Nordic Forces. My velcro nametag replaced the shiny wings the day I graduated training one year ago on my seventeenth birthday. I kept my head held high and my middle finger higher as I passed them.

Classes hadn't started yet, but there would always be individuals eager to knock me out of my position. Which made me question why Ghost didn't threaten or report me. I didn't want to be the typical fighter pilot. I wanted to instruct or become the youngest advisor in Nordic History. I spent every spare moment reading manuals, beating simulators, and studying pilots in the history books to advance my career, to become the best Nordic Airre pilot. That's why I earned higher rankings than most in record time. And also why staying determined was so essential. The higher the ranking, the more freedoms I was afforded, something I'd never had and desired more than anything. Nothing else mattered.

I approached the Ops building and made my way up the steps two at a time to the large metal doors. Students fled the halls and into their classrooms for eight hours of basic military training.

Another set of footsteps fell in line with mine—Ghost. I gave him a darting look over my shoulder. It unnerved me, the way he sneaked up on me, spoke to me as if I was his subordinate he could push around. He was nothing more than a flirt with a stupid *brownnoser* logo.

Irritation boiled up in me. I spun and stopped him in his tracks. "What do you want and why are you following me?"

"Calm down, sweetheart. We need to talk." A deep chuckle came from him. "Seriously. How about dinner? That's all. No strings attached."

I had to swallow back the acid that crept up my throat. Never would I fall for Ghost's charms. *Like hell.* "Never."

Not expecting that answer, Ghost's eyebrows flew up. "What?"

"You need a reality check. Not every female is interested in you," I said dryly. Did he honestly think his good deed was going to change anything between us? "I appreciate you saving my ass this morning. I do. But it changes nothing."

At first, I thought he was going to leave, but then he glanced about for eavesdroppers and then crouched to eye level.

"Even if there are consequences?" he asked.

Yeah, like I was going to fall for that. I leaned in farther to whisper, "I'll take my chances."

Two

Piercing rays of light swept through windows lining the hall, highlighting students in a momentary halo as they ambled down the ivory tiled hallway. Their eyes glanced in my direction as I strode down the corridor with quick steps.

"Jinx, wait up."

I ignored their gazes and Ghost, adding a little extra swing to my hips. In all honesty, I wasn't sure why reporting to squadron so early was all that significant. Modified flight schedules weren't uncommon. Why send us out at all?

A quick vibration stole my thoughts. I slowed down and plucked the comm from my hip, reading the message scrolling across the screen. "Trust no one." A shivery sensation raced down my spine. I eyed the device like a poisonous snake. *What the hell? Was it some sick joke?* The sender ID was blank, and the screen blinked out.

"What do we have there?" Ghost edged closer.

"Huh?" I didn't realize Ghost was sneaking a look over my shoulder. Matter of fact, I forgot about him altogether.

"We? Really?" I asked, cramming the comm back on my hip. "It's none of your damned business," I said stubbornly.

He looked down at me from his 6'4" frame, met my eyes. "Woman, you're maddening," he growled.

"And you're an idiot," I shot back. I was still uncomfortable with the fact that he showed up at Senders Rock, the most unexpected of places. No one, not even the one person I did trust knew where I snuck out to in the mornings.

"Listen," he said, "I know you think I'm just some playboy, but you've got me all wrong. I'm trying to— "

My hand shot up. I pursed my lips. "You're gonna split hell wide open with that lie. I'm not in the mood for this." I didn't think he was pretending to be someone he wasn't, and that's what scared me. No way was I going to allow his persuasive words to manipulate my emotions. I narrowed my eyes, unsure if I should tell him what I thought of him. "Of course, I do, Ghost. You're no different than any other guy out there trying to score and add a notch on your belt. Go ahead and turn me in…" I flicked a glance at the armband. "I'm not going to dinner or continue this discussion with you. I'm unbreakable. Save your charms for one of your harem. Not. Interested," I clarified.

I continued passing classrooms and wound my way through the fleeting students and pilots, Ghost quick on my heels. I turned slightly from the locker room door back to Ghost. "Men's locker rooms are that way." I pointed my finger across the hall. "Unless, you know, you prefer the ladies, which, no doubt, I'm sure you've considered."

"Is that an invitation?" His eyebrows shot up, and then his expression switched to serious like a flip of a switch. "All joking aside, Jinx, I'm going out on a limb here. On the mountain, you took off before I could tell you, but I *have* to speak with you about a private matter." His voice lowered, his body leaned toward mine. "I have reason to believe your life is in danger."

The intensity in his voice almost made me shiver. The whole encounter with Ghost had been weird enough already. "Why are you telling me this? Why should I believe anything you say?" I said a little bitterly.

He shrugged. "I think you should at least hear me out. I can't speak freely here, so can you meet me after the flight, somewhere where we can talk privately. Please."

I tore my gaze from Ghosts. "All right. I'll meet you on one condition. I want to see the evidence, something tangible, and then you leave me the hell alone." I half-closed my eyes. Why, oh why, was I agreeing to this?

"All right." His voice wavered, and then he turned, watching as he disappeared behind the steel door to the men's locker rooms.

I shook the tension from my shoulders and pulled in a calming breath. I had to figure out where the mysterious message came from, and why, if it were true, someone would put a target on my back. Picking out an individual was like throwing darts at a dartboard in the dark. I didn't doubt I had haters, but why would someone warn me to '*trust no one*'? I eyed the device burning a hole in my hip. I shot a nervous glance over my shoulder at the oncoming students. *It could be anyone.*

I wasn't sure what to make of the entire morning, or why he helped me, or why I cared that he did. There was just something about him I had a difficult time processing. My mind said one thing and my body another. I couldn't allow myself to think about him, and the more he came around, the harder it was to brush him off despite my best efforts. Not long ago, I wouldn't have even questioned myself or the way I felt about any guy. It was automatic—they were pigtail pullers and bullies. Now, something new stirred in the pit of my stomach, and I couldn't help but hate that part betraying me. Men were trouble, and Ghost was no exception.

The locker room buzzed with conversations and the slamming of metal doors. Tall rows of tan lockers lined the walls like barriers to the outside world. Long wooden benches placed throughout the room occupied with pilots slipping on anti-G-suits, tying laces and attaching velcro name tags.

I slipped the backpack off my shoulders, carefully setting it down and knelt to rifle through it. Anyone in this room could have sent that message. I scanned the locker room and took a mental note of who was there before I pulled my belongings from my pack, shoving them into the locker.

"Jinx!"

My head shot up. Damn, I was jumpy.

Casper sauntered over, her wild mane sticking out like raging flames against her pale, white skin. A broad smile lit her face as she nudged her hip to mine, sweeping me into a tight bear hug.

"Glad to see you made it back unscathed," she said. "I was beginning to worry about you. Advisor Turner was on the warpath when I passed his office this morning, and I feared you were the reason why." Her burnished blue eyes softened. "I know you're going to do what you want regardless of what I say, but I wish you would stay home until the dust settles with the abductions." I worry about you." Casper's willowy petite frame overshadowed her larger than life personality, radiating exuberance and energy. She was everything I was not and maybe the reason why I liked her so much. She was nothing like me.

I nodded with a polite smile. "I'll consider it."

How could anyone forget the missing trainee's when at every turn there was talk and speculation, signs posted around campus offering a reward for information, a strict curfew hanging over our heads, drones lacing the skies, and ground patrols amped up. And adding to the crazy, Ghost's warning.

An awful mixture of emotions clenched my heart and awakened something inside of me I had not been able to discard. What it was, I was unsure. Frustrated and overwhelmed, I wanted to take off on my bike, isolate myself, and sort out my thoughts.

No surprise Ghost waited for me outside the locker room. He looked up from where he leaned against the wall one leg propped up, head tilted back, and arms crossed. A low grumble escaped my lips as I ignored him and kept in step with Casper.

The squadrons reported two doors down from the locker rooms, just beyond a display case of aviation photos.

We loaded our saddlebags with maps and a few essentials. I noticed Ghost's hulking figure off to the side with Pug and Rucky. Pug lived three doors down from Ghost, and always went after Ghost's leftovers, hoping to score with the brokenhearted. Pug's flat, chubby face was the only one I could see beyond the pilots filling seats. And it wasn't much at that. He was short and squatty with too-long arms. My nose crinkled.

Rucky had a cocky little attitude that brushed off on the guys when they hung out. He rubbed me the wrong way, and I could barely tolerate being around him. Advisors Turner and Sweet seemed to have a keen liking to the critter, probably because he did them special favors. Who knew? I could give two shits less as long as he stayed away from me.

Casper elbowed me lightly. I blinked, clearing my eyes and focused on the maps displayed. Everyone received a flight card. I took the index card given to me by Hook. The metal claw attached to the end of his arm snapped shut. I didn't feel sorry for the metal attachment at the end of his arm. Stealing in Nordic was senseless. Stupid. His punishment met his crime. I glanced down at the white card.

Damn it.

Rucky was flight lead, deliberately planned by Advisor Turner and Sweet I assumed—a small insignificant punishment for the purple stripe in my hair? Taking away my flight lead status pissed me off.

The SOF (supervisor of flying) cleared the pilots to step-to-jets, our dismissal and go-ahead to approach our jets and prepare for flight.

"See you," I said to Casper with a wink, and then pushed out of my chair and grabbed the helmet bag.

"You got it," she replied, with a crooked half smile.

Chair legs squeaked against the tiled floor as the pilots pushed away from their seats. The canvas strap dug deep into my palms, creating red zigzag grooves into the skin. The helmet bag held a parachute harness, survival vest, g-suit, and helmet. Readjusting my grip, I shuffled toward the exit.

Rucky was about ten feet in front of me. He was shorter than the other guys, but he was thick, reminding me of a tree trunk, but squatty like a stump. He got up from the table and attached his card to his leg. He looked up, scanning the room. I busied myself with my bag not wanting to make eye contact. He appeared irritated, or was it nervousness? I dared a glance back. His plump hands rubbed down his face, and he swept up his bag with forced enthusiasm.

Ghost caught my eye. He mouthed the words: *Be careful.* Warmth spread across my cheeks. I looked back over my shoulder. Rucky and Hook were in a heated conversation. I couldn't hear them, but they stood close to one another— veins bulged from the sides of Hook's face. Rucky's turned an alarming shade of red. Hook fisted his one hand tightly against his side. Flexing and fisting.

Beyond Rucky and Hook, Advisor Turner's window blinds shifted, stealing my attention. A partial shadow darkened one side, exposing a scarred cheek through the fissure. My eyes narrowed. The person behind the window slithered back into the shadows. The hair on the back of my neck prickled. The blinds released, shutting me out completely. I creased my brow. The scar triggered something in my memory as if I had seen it before.

I pressed the button on the panel beside the ladder, raising the glass canopy without a mechanical groan. I climbed inside the titanium bathtub, pulled the helmet bag open and dug around for my comm. I sent Casper a message telling her to be extra vigilant. Unaware of the mysterious message I had received, she wasn't aware of the ominous undertone in the brief room.

Be careful up there. Something doesn't feel right. Will explain later.

The wind lashed against the glass windows, and the intensity picked up as large graying clouds crowded the skies, muting the sun's rays. The sky reflected my mood. I felt uneasy and restless.

Rucky climbed into his jet, closed the canopy, sealing himself in. Since he was flight lead, I had to wait on him. My leg bounced. I took a quick look once again at the communicator secured into the side cargo pocket on my arm, hotter than a million suns, and double-checked the fastened shoulder harness, giving a quick tug.

After what seemed like hours, the Crew Chief's gruff voice came through the headset, "Rucky."

Rucky responded. "Check."

As wingman, it was my duty to report in our flight formation to the Crew Chief. "Four-Ship," I confirmed.

Our group consisted of Rucky, Vango, Spade, and me. Vango and Spade were newer releases and lacked the experience

Rucky and I had. But I'd seen them train a handful of times. Spade hung around Rucky on and off base, and regularly went to various hangouts. Vango was quiet. Never said much, but the thin blond guy with a narrow nose was efficient with a target, and that's what mattered.

Supervisor Gest cleared us to taxi out. My heart rate picked up with eagerness. I followed behind my flight lead. The long black tarred surface was smooth under the wheels as they rolled into place at the end of the runway.

"Here we go," I muttered.

Rucky's wheels peeled off down the runway; his speed intensified quickly. Ghost-like fumes blasted out with the powerful thrust. The nose shot into the air as his jet propelled into the darkening sky.

I glanced down at the gauges. I waited for my twenty-second interval, tightened my grip around the plastic-covered steel handle and pressed forward. Small blue lights dotted the runway, growing brighter as the sky darkened. It was like speeding through a tunneling blue vortex. The colors whizzed by faster and faster until the nose rose above the brilliant blue streaks, and surrounded by swelling opaque clouds.

THREE

It was a love like no other. The deep throaty sounds emanated from the jet engines as the four-ship climbed higher in altitude. I leaned my head against the headrest while I breathed in and out through the oxygen mask. I soared far above the ground into the sky, flanking Ruckys' jet. Being up in the atmosphere was like being in another world, another time and another place.

Darkness pressed close as ominous clouds began fusing together in angry masses. I peeked over my left shoulder. Vango was keeping pace within formation. And to the right, large white teeth skirted the nose of Spade's jet. It was ugly. Tacky, really. Very few pilots chose the decorative monstrosity.

We were making good time as we crossed the plains and mountains of Nordic, the city where Commander DeMarco's pretentious mansion was, and closed in on the very edges of the Grande Rouche. The body of water was as vast as it was dangerous. Perilous currents swirled like tunneling tornadoes, pulling many lives into the Rouche's darkest depths, consuming any vestiges within it. The portentous clouds fit my mood as the sky darkened with the brewing storm.

The hour spun by like the undercurrents of time. I looked down at the fuel gauge, concerned a tanker would be needed to refuel in another hour or so. The Voice Message System went off. The dismissive female tone known as "Bitchin' Betty," blasted audio caveats. Blinking red warning lights illuminated the control panel. "You've got to be kidding me," I whispered. I quickly craned my head to the left and right, furiously looking around the mesh netting behind me for Spade and Vango. "Shit. Shit. Shit. Where the hell is he?"

The loud, steady tone blared in my ears, buzzed through my body as every nerve ending turned hyper aware. I was in someone's crosshairs and locked in. It was Spade. *What the hell is he doing?*

Spade quickly broke away. The bleeding warning dissolved into silence. "Not funny, assholes." My heart pounded against my ribs. I twisted to the right, to get a better look at him but all I saw was empty air and angry clouds. Turning to the left, I spotted Spade as he flew up behind Vango. "What the hell is going on?" I shouted, but only my ears could hear. I swung back around; Rucky was no longer in sight. "Shit!" *Never take your eyes off the enemy.* My heart galloped, matching the anxiety quickly building inside my body. Perspiration began seeping from my pores. Sweat laced the palms of my hands, slick against the handle as the reality of the situation hit me. It wasn't a dirty joke or a drill. Spade and Rucky wanted us dead.

My control panel flashed red again. The warning signal went off. A jet was closing in on me. I craned my neck and saw Rucky. He was right on my tail. I pulled into a ninety-degree break turn to defend myself. My rear slid slightly in the seat as I twisted the aluminum tank, and shot-off from Ruckys line of fire.

Spade was in pursuit behind Vango. He was holding his own, but I feared for the newly released pilot as he tried to shake the lecherous shadow that expertly clung to him.

"Son of a…" I maneuvered the jet once again to throw Rucky off. He matched my movements and was difficult to shake. I could do this. "Damn!" I shouted. The red blaring beeps rolled in waves. No way was I going to let that traitor take me or pin me down. If I could wear him down—make him tired or shake him up—his chances of making a mistake or misjudging would be greater. I clicked the UHF mic switch on. "Vango. Do you copy?" Static hissed in my ears. I flipped the switch again and repeated myself with more intensity. "Vango, dammit! Do you copy?"

Static.

Someone severed my communication line. Any transmissions to Nordic Airre air tower and to the other pilots were useless. My stomach lurched. I was on my own. My elbow struck hard against the side of the jet repeatedly until my frustration morphed into hatred. Anger creased my brow and determination set in. This asshole was going to pay. Rucky just messed with the wrong woman.

WITH EVERY STORM cloud, there was a silver lining. I pulled a hard brake right, sweeping back then up behind Rucky. The tides had turned in my favor. My index finger held tight against the little red trigger, the one that would lead to his demise. There would not be another story to play out. I was a fighter to the end.

A long, drawn-out beep buzzed in my ears. I didn't hesitate. I pushed the red trigger. Bullet holes had pelted along the end of Rucky's jet before he pulled away, and out of range. My heart pounded hard, and my stomach clenched. Sweat beads rolled down my temples.

Two streaks of grayish black smoke spewed from one of the other jets. I couldn't tell whose it was or where they were, exactly. Bullets whizzed by streaked with a fiery haze.

The rear of my jet took on a battering of pellets. The sound of metal punctured at a high rate pierced my ears. It had gotten dark so quickly. The storm brewing had claimed the air around us and swallowed the trail of smoke emitting from the jets. Spade had Vango locked in and had elevated above my canopy.

Rucky had taken position behind me again. I pulled, twisted and turned but the constant beep hadn't let up. "Come on!" My blood boiled with anger and frustration. Rucky wasn't giving up, nor was he slowing down. Bullets blasted all around me in steady waves.

Out of nowhere, a fireball streamed by lightning-fast, barely avoiding the nose of my jet. I pulled a hard left. My body jerked against the restraints holding me in. A loud metal screech ripped through the air as another jet clipped my wing, separating it and sending me into a fiery, whirling tailspin.

As the velocity pulled me forward, the impact spun my jet like a Frisbee, round and round. I swallowed down the acid creeping up my throat and screamed. I didn't want to die. Even at the lowest of lows, at the point when I wanted to give up and said I'd rather die, I never really meant it. No one wants to die. And in that final moment, you fight like hell. That was how I was going down—a fighter until the end.

My sweat-slicked finger squeezed the little red trigger with all I had and released all the white-hot anger and fear within me. Bullets fired out in at unstoppable speed, penetrating through Rucky's jet. Shards of glass erupted from his canopy and a brilliant burst of flames engulfed his aircraft.

I had no idea how long I spun uncontrollably or how I managed to grasp the handles attached on the side of the seat. My jet would never land, but I succeeded and ejected from the blazing inferno around me, rocketing toward the Grand Rouche.

The air swept me up in an instant, the breath from my lungs stolen. My parachute sprang out, and I soared downward toward the watery grave. Chunks of metal and other unknown debris plummeted from the stormy sky, splinters of glass and gassy fumes burnt my nose and tore holes in the flight suit like sharp talons.

Had I been the only one to make it out alive? In the heat of the battle, I hadn't noticed the coordinates of the location. The conflict ensued for so long. Dodging the cacophony of bullets, I had no idea where I was. All I knew was that my world ruptured, and the patina of the Rouche waited below.

FOUR

I wasn't alone.

A killer screech echoed in my head. Large blinding lights pulsed behind my eyes. My head felt like it was going to explode into a million pieces of human shrapnel. I wanted to scream, grip my hair and pull until the pain subsided, but my body wouldn't obey my commands. Hushed voices joined the noise hammering under my skull. I wanted to shut-them-the-hell-up, and for the cleaving pain to go away. The noise was too much. The intense waves of nausea were too much. I bit my lip to keep from crying out, but a whimper escaped my lips.

A mixture of salty air and smoke permeated my senses. I kept my eyes closed, pretending to be safe in my own bed, but I knew I wasn't. A sense deep in my core told me I'd not be returning to Nordic. Shivers danced along my arms, down to my feet. Where was I? Who was here with me—wherever *here* was?

"Do you think she escaped? She could be a spy, Luke. We should have let her drown. We have to find out if she's with the men in the cove. If she is..."

"Enough," a man hissed. "I know what you're thinking. We know nothing and until she's strong enough we wait," he whispered.

The floor creaked under the weight of someone in the room. A door slammed. I lay still and quiet. Would I be tortured if they knew where I came from? Who I was? Use me for leverage? I couldn't think. It hurt. My bones hurt. My skin hurt.

I willed my pinky to slowly rub against the scratchy material beneath me, get a better feel for what irritated my skin. Wool. A blanket of wool covered me. The throbbing continued and a pulsing bulb of torment pounded away in my skull. It was all too much, and the darkness overtook me.

MY EYES CRACKED open to slits, but could see nothing beyond the flicker of a fires shadow licking the wall. Ripples of warmth caressed my backside, but did nothing for the coldness that ran deep to my bones.

A steady grinding noise filled my ears as if metal grated against rough stone over and over. Had I had the energy, I would've showed them where to shove it. The sound irked me. I didn't know how long I could go on before I passed-out again. Bordering between consciousness and the black silence,

I wanted the pain to go away. I wanted to die.

My chest shot forward of its own accord. Vulgar retching noises pulsed in my ears. It had been me. My stomach muscles tensed and bile rose from deep down. Warm liquid laced with acid and salt erupted like a volcano, burning and spraying out before me. Tears rolled down my cheeks. I clutched my stomach until the heaves subsided, and collapsed onto the cot.

THEY WERE TALKING about me. Hushed voices rose above a crackling fire. The sooty smell teased my nose, warmth licked my backside, and the flickering light bled through my eyelids. How long had I been out? A haze skirted my thoughts, but I was able to comprehend with more clarity than before.

They spoke quietly, but there were more than the previous two voices. Luke, was it? The name rolled off my tongue with vague uncertainty.

My backside ached, matching the throb in my head, but the cramping in my stomach was torture. It was just pain, but the funny thing about pain was it demanded your attention. I remembered retching, the dry heaves shaking my body. I grazed my cracked dry lips. I was so thirsty. I had to move. I had to get up.

The stiff cot was no better than the damned floor. A shot of whisky would do the trick. Then suddenly, I thought of Ghost. I told him I'd meet him after the flight. Would he come looking for me? *A comrade shot me. It wasn't a training mission, it was an execution. Oh God, where am I?* I'm breathing deeper, my chest rising and falling quickly, as panic crept in. I felt hot and sick, and I wanted to cry. I tucked the blanket up under my chin a little snugger as I mulled over everything that had happened and prayed a search party would find me.

"You're awake." It was a statement, not a question. Warm minty breath touched my face. "You need to drink." I opened my eyes, my vision blurry, and focused on a pocked metal cup held between thick, rough fingers, inching toward me. The fingers belonged to a man. White scars snaked across his fingers and hand like veins of a river branching off on a map.

"Can you hear me? Drink," said the gruff voice. "It's mandatory life fuel. It will help."

I bristled. Would he drug me or add a little something in there to finish what Rucky had started? The words *"Trust no one,"* flashed in my mind. Whoever had sent that comm clearly knew danger was in my future.

"I'm not deaf." I paused." You first," I said, my voice scratchy and weak. I cleared my throat and scooted up with painful slow movements. A faint moan escaped my lips. A haze of golden light traced the man's broad shoulders. But he was no angel, I was sure of that.

He nudged the cup closer. I turned my head, denying his offer. There was no way I would accept that drink as much as my mind urged me to take it. I fought the impulse to rip the mug from his hands and guzzle the minty-smelling liquid.

"Maybe I want to die. I was supposed to die."

"Just take it," he demanded in a not-so-kind tone. "The

mint will help sooth your throat. Now drink it."

"You can go fu…"

"I wouldn't finish that sentence if I were you," he said. "I can turn away, leave you in here to wilt, or you can drink this and help yourself. It's your choice. Either way, I don't care."

My head craned around, eyes narrowed to slits as I stared at the man. A few days of stubble was noticeable, the tapered light shadowed the rest of his features. He hadn't said another word. The metal cup clinked against the ground as he set it down and then turned on his heel to leave.

"Wait," I said, before the piercing light of the opened door swallowed him, vanishing from sight.

"Damn it." I flopped back onto the cot, wincing from the shooting pain down my body, and flung my arm over my eyes. "What am I going to do," I whispered to myself. I didn't know where I was or whose company I was in. Everything felt wrong. I slammed my other fist hard against the makeshift bed. I wanted to scream, to lash out.

My mouth watered—the tea was seducing my taste buds. Against my better judgment I sat up, let out a huff of air and scooped up the mug. It was warm to the touch. I sniffed the contents. Steamy mint tea rose up, dampening my face. The smell was wonderful, and my stomach growled in response. I pulled in a sip, and then consumed the rest.

They must have slipped something into the tea. I had fallen back to sleep, and when I woke up, there was nothing but inky blackness surrounding me. The light that once circled the door was gone. Far off laughter echoed. The rumble of a truck engine sounded, followed by a door closing. I sat up, trying to adjust to the darkness and swung my legs over the side of the cot. I let out a breath. My body wasn't as sore anymore, and I managed to push off the edge with both hands. Cool wood greeted my feet as I shuffled across the floor toward the door. I reached out, probing for obstacles.

Tink went the metal cup as my foot knocked it over on its side. "Crap." I sluggishly moved forward, hoping I wouldn't encounter another object in my path.

"She lives. Where do you think you're going?" The same husky voice with an odd accent I recognized from earlier.

"Would you rather I piss myself?" I shot back. I knew nothing about this guy and yet, here I was, again with him. Was it Luke? The man who watched over me?

My stance loosened. I wasn't afraid of him. He had ample opportunity to hurt me and hadn't. It was still too dark to see clearly, but I could just make out the silhouette of a hearth and a chair in the corner. A thick warm hand wrapped loosely around my arm without warning. I jerked back in response, lifting my other arm swiftly. My right hook made contact against his rock-hard jaw. His head lurched to the side, and hair fell from a ponytail in the back. "Don't' touch me!"

"Shit." He released my arm. But then with quick, deft moves, he wrapped me in a gorilla hold, pasting my arms against my sides.

"Let. Me. Go." I tried to buck against him, losing strength as I struggled.

"You're pretty damn feisty, aren't you?"

His body heat enveloped me. A drop of liquid rolled down my cheek. A metallic tang pierced my senses. *His blood or mine?* I repeated myself, squirming and kicking but getting nowhere in his iron grip.

"Stop fighting me. I'm not going to hurt you."

"And why should I believe you?" I said between ragged breaths.

"If I was, don't you think I would've by now? Hmmm?" His warm breath reached my ear. "I'm going to slowly ease my arms away. If you try and attack me again, this time I won't be so nice. Understood?"

I denied him a response, and refused to give him the satisfaction of obeying his command. He must have taken my silence as confirmation. His arms loosened their viselike grip, easing away bit by bit. I jerked back, twisting so that he wouldn't be able to hold on. I couldn't see his face, but I wanted to. I wanted to see his expression when I turned and stomped hard on his foot, hefted my knee into his groin, and made a final blow to his face. But he *hasn't* hurt or threatened me. So why did I feel like my life balanced on a delicate scale? One wrong move, the scale would tip, and I'd die.

Maybe if I played the part of an obedient prisoner, a chance to escape would present itself. I'd find a way home, stop Rucky if he had survived, and figure out how to move on with my life. He stood tall and sure, dabbed a cloth beneath his nose and said, "There's a john through the door over there." He pointed to the far wall behind the cot. "Try anything like that again and I'll have to bind you up. Assuming you'll be on good behavior,

I'll give you some privacy."

I was caught between him and the walls of the closed-in room, I had nowhere to go, and was too weak to fight or run. For a moment I stood frozen in place, waiting for him to make an advance, but instead, he hesitated, then turned on his heel and left. The door clicked shut behind him. I exhaled.

FIVE

I sat silently on the edge of the cot, and stared down at the bowl of stew in my hands. I hadn't been able to get any information out of the man, nor had he gotten anything useful from me. It was more torture than not, playing the elusive information game of tug-of-war. I wouldn't bend. He wouldn't either. All I knew was his name was Luke, his hand was scarred, he wasn't alone outside of these suffocating walls, and he didn't trust me...yet.

He sat in the chair across from me, elbows on knees, fingers laced together, face hidden behind the shadows. He never showed his face. There was never light, only a hazy dimness I couldn't adjust my eyes to beyond where his feet rested. The air was thick with humidity and warm.

The chair squeaked as his body shifted. I imagined his hair pulled back in a low ponytail, skimming the edges of his shirt.

He broke the silence. "Were you alone? Were there others with you?"

The same rhetoric every time he sat watching me eat. Why would he care? Did he or his people find Vango, Spade, or Rucky? Were they in a locked room being interrogated, too?

"Does it exhaust you listening to yourself talk?" My voice came out raspy and dry as if I'd swallowed a spoonful of sand. The bed squeaked as my leg bobbed up and down.

"Just answer the question!" He slammed his palms against the armrests. " Listen," he said urgently, lowering his voice, "I've seen that flight suit before, I know where you're from, and I want to help you. But first, I need to know...was there anyone else with you?"

What I wanted to say was screw you, but something in his voice made me curious what in the hell he was searching for and why he'd want to help me. I did want to trust he was telling the truth, but then my mind flashed back to the communicator screen. *Trust no one.*

"What makes you think for a second I'd tell you anything?" I asked, feeling brave. He could've been collaborating with Rucky and Spade for all I knew. It made sense. Maybe he was waiting for them, but instead, found me. "You've kept me locked up, offered zero information as to where I am or who you are..." I placed the bowl on the wooden floor by my feet a little too hard, "or why you'd want to help me. How do you know I didn't steal this suit and strategically plant myself where I'd be found?" My chest was rising and falling too quickly as a spike of anger surged through my veins.

"Our time is running short. The others will be back soon. Discovering you was accidental. You're lucky I was with them when they spotted your parachute floating in the Rouche. When we pulled you from the tangle of rope and nylon, I carried you to the beach. Then performed resuscitation to expel the water from your lungs and color to your blue face. I saved your life. You owe me. I *know* you're from Nordic, so tell me...were you alone or not?"

I didn't know why I felt compelled to tell him the truth. I focused all my energy on what I was about to say, and told myself not to think about it. Because if I wanted to get out of there, I had to make him believe I was worth the risk.

"No. And...yes. The other jet—my comrade, Rucky—burned before hitting the water. I swear."

He released a heavy breath as if relief flooded him, and cleared his throat. Off in the distance the rumble of a truck engine grew louder.

"Shit," the guy said, swiftly pushing up from the chair. "Time has run out."

What did that mean for me? He seemed confused, upset, and unsure of himself as his boots thudded against the floor. He paced quickly to the door and back like a trapped animal. I knew what I had to do. The element of surprise was my only opportunity of escaping.

A loud thump and groaning struck the air. I sent a silent *thank you* up to the heavens for my hand to hand combat class. I hurried away, but my movement was lazy and slow. I could feel the presence of a wall in front of me. It was the closed-in claustrophobic kind of sense, where it's dark, but the darkness deepened and I knew I was there. My hands scurried along the walls surface. Didn't these people use anything other than wood? My hand whacked against a lever of steel, and my fingers fumbled to work it.

I could still hear groans coming from the man. I jiggled the metal contraption, hoping it would open. "Come on," I muttered. Beads of sweat danced along my hairline. With one hefty push, the metal rod slid along the door and I pushed against it. I stumbled onto my trembling hands and knees, my body jolted as it smacked against the earth. I shook my clouded head as I crab-crawled to get up. Dew-coated leaves and debris slid around beneath me.

There were no stars to light my way, only a dash of moonlight filtered through dense fog that blanketed the ground. Urgency to get away bore down heavy into the pit of my soul. The ground beneath me seemed to elevate the farther I went, straining my already aching muscles. I snuck a glance over my shoulder, but it was useless. The night's fog swallowed the path behind me. The engine's rumble ceased. A door slammed shut. My head swam as fatigue wrestled my anxiety. I ran as hard as I could. If they caught up to me, I wouldn't stand a chance. My breath tore at my chest as I pushed myself faster.

My bare feet were cold, my fingers scraped against the roughness of a tree I skirted and then another. Rocks poked and prodded my skin as I ascended what must have been another hill. My energy was consumed with effort as I demanded myself to keep running. Branches tugged and pulled at my clothes and hair.

I squinted against the darkness, barely making out a bowed, low-lying trunk five paces ahead of me. *Keep moving, don't give up,* I said to myself over and over. But I wanted to collapse and melt into the ground. My arms and legs were numb and I couldn't continue. I slumped down on the soft ground, the ridges bit into my skin as I leaned against the fallen tree.

No. Get up.

My head rolled back onto the bark, eyes heavy. My breaths were shallow and labored.

Casper would have been proud of how hard I fought. A weak smile tipped my cracked lips thinking of my friend. I wondered where she was right now. Was she nestled beneath her covers, sound asleep? I could only dream of being in my bed across the hall from her. We were assigned as roommates in our apartment and our friendship formed quickly. We could thank Ghost for that one. His apartment was across the small courtyard, our sliders faced one another, and he did just about anything to annoy us—a new girl giggling in the night as their menacing heels clanked against the sidewalk as they came and went past our door. And intentionally leaving his blinds open just enough to see him walk past with only a bath towel draped loosely around his hips. It had been our cheap entertainment.

"Please find me, someone. Please," I whispered softly. A single tear rolled down my cheek and I closed my eyes and steeled myself. My chest rose and fell, matching my slow, tired breaths.

"Okay, I can do this." When I opened them, I rolled over

onto my hands and knees, using the log to brace myself, and inhaled a deep breath. My mind and body wasn't done torturing me, but beyond the pain, in some distant part of my brain I was fully aware that I could be a dead lifeless forgotten body lost at sea. After a long moment, I pushed myself away from the tree. Animals chirped and chattered all around, twigs snapped under my feet.

I remembered Ghost saying he had reason to believe my "life was in danger," what seemed like a lifetime ago, back by the locker rooms of Nordic Airre, getting ready for our flight training. If only I'd known then what I knew now.

After wondering around aimlessly, a stone overhang was where I settled, the night surrounding me like a cloak. Pulling my knees to my chest, I curled into a ball until the silence of sleep took me, cancelling out the world.

SIX

ight pierced through large tropical leaves as they gently swayed in the breeze shifting the rays. I reached up, kneading my stiff neck. I groaned. My arm was a weak imitation of a pillow. I looked around the surrounding emerald vines blending into the cacophony of tangled branches and rustling, overgrown vegetation. My feet were bare and caked with what must be dirt mixed with my own blood. Scratches reached from toe to ankle, red and angry. There were wounds that no one could see. But I felt them inside.

My heart ached.

My fingers gently skimmed over the scrapes, wiping away at the dirt around them. My feet exposed, stripped of my boots. My captors had taken them away, but not my will to survive. I may have lost my possessions, but I'd never lose myself. That was something no one could ever steal. It was a piece of me, my soul. I was a survivor. "I'll find a way out of here," I whispered, voice barely noticeable to my own ears. The words came out gruff and scratchy against my raw throat. Did they think I wouldn't try to escape? I scoffed. They knew nothing about me...or did they?

Looking down at my outstretched legs, my flight suit had small rips and tears scattered around the gray material. The velcro call sign still clung to the left chest pocket. "They know my name," I murmured to myself. "Shit." My fingers ran across the embroidered letters. JINX. The name said it all—What irony.

A loud grumbling erupted from my stomach. I couldn't recall the last time I had eaten. Forcing the thought of food aside, I looked around through the hanging vines and the drooping lacey greens. We didn't have tropical plants in Nordic or vines streaming from branch to branch like coiling snakes. So where was I? Without my helmet bag, I was lost. The maps of the islands were inside and more than likely rested on the bottom of the Rouche, along with my jet.

The events of the routine fight rolled through my mind. I was assigned second in a four-ship with Rucky as lead and Vango and Spade in the rear. Spade attacked Vango. Rucky had attacked me. My plane had been clipped by Vango's as it swiftly descended toward the Grande Rouche—shot down by one of our own, Spade. I blasted Rucky's jet, turning it into a falling blaze. But...I couldn't recall ever seeing Spade's jet in any form of distress. Had he escaped the dogfight? Had Rucky or Vango? They could have ejected. But my last memory was hitting the water. I shook my head, hoping for some form of clarity, something I could hold onto. But it was useless. My memory was a clean slate. There was nothing beyond the choppy waters of the Rouche.

Brows pinched, I mulled over the details over and over and I got the same result every time—Spade had escaped unscathed. He had to have. But would he go back to Nordic? My pulse quickened, ignoring the grumble in my stomach. I fisted the soft dirt beneath my palms, unleashing the hate I felt and the anger pent up. I'm severed from the world, from everything I had ever known, and sickened because I knew I was on my own. *I was on my own.*

I swiped away the saucy tears tipping the rim of my eyes, still shaken by Rucky and Spade's heedless decision at attempted murder. And for all I knew, Vango didn't survive. I did though, and I wouldn't give up until I uncovered the meaning of it. I was reminded, all over again, why I couldn't trust anyone. Not even my own comrades.

I contemplated my situation, and it occurred to me I was victim to an unguarded place. Despite the aches, I pushed myself up; dusted off my rear and set pace away from the rocky overhang. The humid air pressed down. I unzipped the suit, pulled my arms and legs carefully from each tattered sleeve and tied it gently around my waist, grateful for the tank top and light leggings underneath. Adjusting the knot around my stomach, I stared hard at my dirt caked nails, and slender lines and jagged cuts on my hands and skin.

Unknown creatures prattled. But it was so quiet, even my

thoughts seemed to echo. A little furry animal swung through the air extending a gangly arm for the next vine, gliding along melodically. Large vibrant flowers dotted among the greenery stood out like white lilies in a murky pond. Trees loomed high as far as the eye could see. This land was unusual and mysterious, and my curiosity was piqued.

My fingers traced the edge of a waxy leaf, the color of Nordics' spring sprouts. I rarely went beyond the limits of Sender's Rock, past the edges of the mountainous base into the cities where industrial buildings' smokestacks burped dark pollutants into the air, high-rises blocked and shadowed the warm sun from faces, and the suffocating population. My free time was my time, and a good portion was spent on the seat of my motorcycle cruising the country back roads.

I couldn't ignore the ache my hunger brought on. It twisted tight in my gut. I'm not one of those people who needs to eat as soon as I wake up, but the hunger would make me sick eventually if I didn't find something soon. I stepped over more fallen limbs and brushed away corkscrew vines as I continued to move on, stopping periodically to listen for any recognizable sounds or catch a breath.

Something lean and brown slithered across my path and vanished into the undergrowth. For several heart-pounding seconds, I stood motionless, feeling my chest squeeze and my lungs tighten. Sweat beads formed and framed my face. I brushed back my damp hair relieved slightly by the soft breeze that kicked up. There were not any beaten down paths or roads to guide, only lush vegetation to weave around and tromp through.

I wandered around, hoping I would find food or a water source sooner than later. I wouldn't give up hope. I let the loss of the new pilot, my comrade in flight, fuel my determination and move forward. Time passed by with swirling thoughts. Repeatedly my mind replayed the events and the tragic loss.

And then I thought of the trainees who vanished a month ago, and the Nordic Airre four-ship that had been lost about ten months ago. No one knew what happened to the pilots or ever spoke of it after Commander DeMarco released a statement saying it was a 'tragic loss' and blamed it on 'faulty communication mics and control panels inside the jets'. The whole accident seemed hush hush, as if forbidden to speak of it. Now, I couldn't help but wonder if they were deliberately shot down, and on some remote island or country, held captive like me. It had been pillow talk between suite mates, but silenced immediately on base like a bad plague.

"My comm," I whispered. The sudden reminder halted my steps. I tore away at the knot from my waist dropping to my knees with ravaged hands. "The cargo pocket. It has to be there." I pulled the flap up, popping the little round button off in the process. A small hard device sprung from the suit, cradled in my hands. I pulled it next to my chest and held it there for a moment. My eyes closed for an instant. I clasped the device to my chest tighter, tipping my chin up toward the sky in prayer.

"Thank you," I said aloud.

I pressed a finger to the small power button on the top left of the palm sized device. Nothing. I pressed it again, harder, willing the small screens green backlight come to life. The comm didn't work. It was as dead as the traitors were going to be when I got ahold of them. If I could get my hands on a few tools, something sturdy and flat, I could work on the device and only trust it would be capable to transmit an S.O.S. I could only hope, but hope was receding like a bad hairline.

I took a moment to breathe, and gather my bearings. A gruff noise broke my thoughts. I froze. The grumble of an engine resonated, silencing the forest animals. My breathing hitched at the implication. I swept up the jumpsuit, tying it securely in place and tucked the comm inside my bra, keeping it close. My pulse pounded hard against my throat.

I quickly tore off strips of the sleeves, wrapped and tied them securely around my scratched, raw feet and crept cautiously toward the noise. Male voices grew louder, becoming more than conversation. They spoke with clipped words full of tension and urgency. Was it Luke and his groupies looking for me? I darted behind a nearby tree and crouched low, peeking around it. A group of men surrounded a tank of a truck, but too far for a clear view. I blended into the shadows, creeping low to the ground from one tree to the next not daring to get any closer from there. I stared through patchy trees and saw a dilapidated shack barely visible among the undergrowth climbing up the sides.

A stocky built guy approached the front entrance with heavy steps. His hair, cropped low, was a lighter shade of brown. He looked to be in his late forties to early fifties by the deep creases and silver lining his hair. In one swift motion, his foot shot out, kicking in the door with a booted foot. I cringed at the sudden movement and jarring noise and quickly pulled back behind the tree with my hand over my mouth.

The rotted door flew from its hinges, crashing down hard. I caught my breath and dared another look. Two men flanked the aggressor. Boss Man motioned them ahead. They rushed into the cabin with machine guns aimed and ready. They wore dark pants and tops. The shirts harbored a thick blue stripe around the right bicep. My eyes squinted, my memory taking in every last detail of these men. There were five. All wore matching clothes...except one. As he stepped away from the truck, an additional yellow stripe layered above the blue stood out like a beacon. He raised his head, uncovering an ugly scar trailing across his face.

Something about him seemed faintly familiar, like I'd seen him before. Did he resemble someone from my past? I had never seen that man before. *I couldn't have, could I?* They moved with purpose sweeping through and around the cabin. One man came out, guarding the military truck as well as the perimeter. They obviously weren't trying to be quiet. Crashing sounds and shattering glass echoed in the silence of the jungle. It was all I could hear besides my throbbing ears matching my pulse.

The man whom I assumed was the leader pulled out from the cabin, swiping a fat hand down his branded face.

"What is it, sir?" One guy asked. It was the slender man guarding the vehicle. Concern laced his tone.

The scarred man replied, "She's not here. We don't stop

until I have her. Let's move out." He proceeded to exit the creaky porch followed by his two lackeys. One after the other, they all climbed inside the truck and tore out of sight.

I slid back against the tree slowing my breaths. *Were they looking for me? I was being hunted down?* "I have to get out of here," I breathed. I waited until the orange and red of the setting sun to bleed through the branches before I detached myself from the hard bark and shield of the tree.

I approached the rickety old cabin, sweeping my eyes around the area slowly. It had been raised off the jungle floor, perched up on cement blocks. The cabin seemed to have sturdy bones. I did a quick sweep around again before I stepped onto the porch. It creaked in protest as my full weight bore down on the unbalanced wood. Greenish-brown spindly vines wove around the boards and even a few had separated from the rest leaving holes.

I gripped the wooden doorframe, quickly pulling my hand away. I peered inside and back to the doorframe where a chunk of splintered wood had been pushed back and had poked my hand. Upon a closer inspection, I spotted whittled letters poking out from beneath the shard. I brushed away dust and the dangling piece of wood to see the deep etching. G.D.P.S. I studied the letters, wondering who they belonged to.

A burst of mildewed air burned my nose. Cobwebs strung from corners. A small handmade table with mismatched chairs had been upturned off to one side. Pushed against the far wall is a thin droopy mattress on a frameless single bed, stripped of coverings. And beside that, on the floor, a grubby-looking sheet. My eyes pinched; a makeshift kitchen of sorts appeared at the end.

I stepped around the fallen door, working my way inside. A wooden plank held up by four posts created a counter, and an old wood stove tucked in next to it. A small partition blocked the view and I was curious what was on the other side. I stepped around a fallen chair, bent down and righted it. My nose crinkled at the musty smell enveloping the room. Dust particles glimmered like confetti as the light trickled in through a small window above the tipped over furniture. A tickle in my nose caused three consecutive sneezes to erupt. I wrapped my arms around my stomach, holding it against the strained muscles. It was so quiet and in that moment, I felt utterly alone.

Shattered pieces of jagged glass lay strewn across the dusty floor. I stepped around the glass, and into the tiny kitchen, noticing a small cupboard against the partition. The place was a mess, a complete disaster. The soldiers left nothing untouched except for a hand built cupboard. I pulled the handle and it squealed in protest. My eyes widened at the canned goods stacked on shelves. I grabbed a couple hungrily wiping off the dust. A small metallic object with a sharp point on one end pulled my attention. I grabbed it, puncturing a hole into the metal can. It pulled back without much effort. Preserved pineapple replaced the musty odor of the room and I tipped the can to my lips hastily. Smooth fruity juice flowed into my mouth. The sweet liquid flooded my taste buds, and it was all I could do to not lick the can getting every last drop remaining.

I finished off two cans of pineapple, and a can of greens. I had to stop myself even though I wanted so badly to keep going. The sweetness of the fruit was addicting. But I knew I would get sick if I didn't cut myself off. Whoever had lived here had to have been gone for a long time by the looks of the uninhabited cabin. But why leave the food?

Searching around every nook and crevice of the cabin, I ended up with a pair of leather boots, a size too big, and a knapsack I made from torn cloth. I stuffed the bag with smaller cans.

A small hand-sized switch knife was wedged between the counter and the stove. I pressed my hip against the hard surface, inching it back, sweeping up the wedged knife. I rolled the object around between my fingers. It was cool to the touch. A combination of dark wood and steel rested in the palm of my hand. My finger ran over the smooth polished steel and engraved initials, G.A.D.

I wondered whom the knife belonged to, and if it was once a treasured keepsake, one that had been misplaced or lost. Depositing it into my bag, I combed through the rest of the house, what little there was of it. Worried the soldiers would come back, I gathered up the small amount of supplies and left, not looking back.

I didn't know what direction to go or *where* I'd go. It was a blank canvas to explore. Getting far away from the compound would be in my best interest. I was curious about those men, who they worked for, and who they were seeking out. A thought struck me. My brain seemed to come alive from the nourishment, and logic set in. "The comm," I said.

I pulled the comm out from my bra, turning it over to the back side. Setting the rag-bag beside me, I dug through it, taking out the knife. The tip of the knife fit seamlessly into the groove of the bolt holding the comm in one piece and twisted. After multiple attempts, the bolt loosened and pulled away. A hint of corrosion caked around metal pieces inside the device. I wasn't a Techy. I could fix my bike, but a device? I took a closer look. Squinting, pulling the comm closer to my face, I gazed over the intricate little pieces. Green and red tiny wires crisscrossed attaching to flat metal squares. A putty-like substance adhered to the inside corner as if someone had tampered with the communication device. Upon closer inspection, faint tracings of half-moon arches embedded in the charcoal putty with a circular microchip within it. *That's odd.* I cut a small piece of tattered material hanging from my suit, and carefully wiped away flakes of corrosion. Everything seemed intact, yet, the small battery light on the top edge didn't light up. I wiggled the wires, hoping for a small miracle—that maybe it would miraculously spring to life and produce a signal to call for help.

The salty water from the Rouche affected the instruments power, shorting out the current. My knee bounced as I bit my bottom lip, starring down at my lifeline as water pooled in my eyes. I pressed my fingers into the corner of my eyes and took a deep calming breath. What was I going to do?

I pulled myself together after multiple mental pep talks, replaced the parts and screws and placed it back into my bra where it was safe. This was the only piece of home I had and I wanted to keep it close to my heart.

Silhouettes grew dense as the light faded all around me. The humid air kept me warm. I walked aimlessly for hours through the now darkened jungle. Loneliness had never been an impediment. I was content on my own...until now. My heart ached thinking about home. I missed my comrades and the normalcy of my daily routine. The sounds of the throaty A-80's, pushing top speeds on my motorcycle, and even the flirty giggles emanating from Ghost's apartment.

I never thought I would deliberate that—but I had, and I missed all of it. I remembered Ghost's big chocolate brown eyes that stared into mine, and his golden-kissed skin. His lopsided dimpled smile, as annoying as it was, and the way his eyes roamed over my body on Senders Rock. I laughed at the ridiculousness of it all.

SEVEN

Silver streaks edged the clouds and muted a long dirt path beyond the suffocating jungle. It stood out against the all-green backdrop. Two jeeps with years of wear sat quietly adjacent to a cement block building on the north side of the makeshift airstrip. I hunched down, shielded by large leafy branches. I walked quickly, skirting around the open perimeter, within the shadows. There was a small hanger just south of the building structure, its metal roof rusted from exposure to the brackish, humid climate. The too large boots proved a difficult to maneuver in quietly, heavier than any I'd worn in Nordic. I wondered whose boots they were and why anyone left them behind in the modest hidden shack.

Staying a safe distance from the building, I waited, brushing back stray, damp strands of hair from my forehead. A quick shadow passed a trio of windows lining the wall closest to where

I was bunkered down. A gut feeling or an instinct told me I was on an island somewhere way out into the Rouche. This land reeked of salt and sea, of moisture rich earth, and sweet nectar.

Two tall men stepped out into the muted haze and stopped beside one of the jeeps. Both men were sizable and wore a uniform, but neither matched the men who invaded the cabin. One had on an all-black cargo pants, a fitted short-sleeved shirt with a golden patch on the front left breast barely visible at my angle. His hat cast a shadow over his face and I could barely make out his lips moving. Who were these men and who did they work for? Could they be a rebel group or some sort of secret society that Commander DeMarco kept silent about?

A brief handshake ended their discussion, and one of the uniformed men took one last drag from his cigarette, and retreated to the building. But the other, the man in all black, stole a glance at the retreating man. He bore an expression of determination on his face not hidden behind a hat, and shot a look in my direction before disappearing into the jeep. My hands shot up to cover my mouth. *Impossible.* I couldn't accept what I witnessed—dark chocolate eyes I dreamt of a few days past...Ghost Allen.

I continued to huddle behind the shielding branches; hands pressed against my mouth, and closed my eyes. The ebbing rumble of the Jeep was all but a faint memory now. *How could it be? Was Ghost working with those people? Was he conspiring against Nordic? Working with Rucky? No.* I shook my head. *It was my mind toying with me. Just someone who resembled him, that's all.*

I sat frozen in the waning peachy light, using a tree trunk for a backrest, picking at my nail cuticles in thought. The jungle creatures stirred restlessly. Long caws echoed from colorful birds as they took flight from their perches. Wings flapped with urgency as they rose into the sky.

A snap of a twig broke my trance. My eyes widened and my breath hitched. The sound was very close. I couldn't move, afraid to be seen, and most likely was already.

A large hand clamped over my mouth. I panicked, and lost all train of rational thought as I kicked my leg from under me, thrashing against him. I tugged at the hand casing my mouth, and connected a blow to their shin. "Shh, quit fighting me," a male voice rasped as he pulled me against his crouched body. I tried to scream, but the hand muffled the sound. I thrashed against the strong clutch, barely making any progress.

My teeth clamped down on the attackers fingers. My arm slipped from his grip and I rammed my elbow into his kidney. Our bodies lurched forward, but the man recovered, and slid an arm around my waist. My arms shot out breaking the fall, pinning me beneath his massive body and the debris covered ground. Scratchy earth coated my cheek.

My back was against his hard chest, his other arm wrapped around my waist, digging into my ribs. I felt desperation rising as entrapment suffocated me. I couldn't pull in a deep breath; my lungs struggled for air with his weight pressing hard against me.

"Jinx, stop!" the husky voice said close to my ear.

My body iced over and shivers raced down my spine. I knew that deep voice. *But it couldn't be. Was it really him?* My heart pounded as I held still in Ghost Allen's arms.

"That's right," he said. "I came for you," he whispered into my ear.

A million thoughts raced through my mind and only one was clear as the sky—Ghost wasn't a figment of my imagination. How ignorant I was. I saw him and convinced myself it was a look-alike, not the immensely annoying flirty pilot from Nordic because there was no way he could be here, right?

"Can't...breathe."

The heaviness slipped away and I laid there in disbelief. The words were stolen from my lips. They opened, but nothing came out. My chest throbbed, a pang of hurt traced my heart. I rolled myself over and wiped the dirt from my face with shaking hands. My chest was still heaving as I looked into Ghost's brown eyes and thought of the struggle and the words he spoke moments ago. *"I came for you."* Ghost didn't move, just stared into my eyes. I broke the stare, peering down and back up, taking in the playboy who said 'he came for me.'

"I'm glad you're okay," he whispered, gazing down on me. "I was worried that maybe someone had already gotten to you."

I didn't tell him how scared I was of the exact same thing. "How did you find me?" was all I managed to whisper. A cyclone of emotions twirled in my head. Seeing a familiar face did nothing to calm my nerves. I couldn't wrap my mind around the idea of Ghost in front of me or how he could have found me—one person in what seemed to be a very large jungle.

His intense brown eyes searched mine as he rubbed his neck. "There's a lot to explain, Jinx, but now isn't the time. We need to get out of here and *then* I will answer all of your questions..."

I thought I was more perceptive than most. But there I was, deliberating whether or not to trust him. "Now," I interrupted. "How is it possible you are here, standing in front of me when I have been tracking through this god-awful place for god-knows-how-long and you just magically appear, like a damned dream?"

Ghost stepped into my personal space. "Jinx, we have to get out of here now. I stole a truck and I'd like to be far away from here when they come looking for it," he said, so calmly I wanted to rip out my hair.

In a rush, I realized that what he said had everything to do with a much larger picture than miraculously finding me against the odds. The look of urgency on his face was unmistakable, but I still wasn't convinced. "You must think I'm ignorant," I scoffed. "I'm not going anywhere with a traitor." I nailed him with slit eyes and began to laugh. I heard the madness in it.

There was no other explanation. I needed to hear him to tell me Spade was been taken into custody, Rucky's lifeless body was found floating in the Rouche, and Commander DeMarco sent out a search party to find Vango and me. I wanted to dump myself into his arms and release the flood of tears I had held back for countless days. Maybe I'd been cursed to live out some hellish sentence. And I wondered if it was possible to get past the ghosts that haunted me. Nevertheless, every time I closed my eyes, and saw Rucky's face, and Spade's, it reminded me why I was there in the first place. I wasn't dreaming. This terrible thing that happened was another nightmare I'd never wake up from. I was living it.

His expression was unreadable, but when a callused hand circled around mine, I spun around, punching into the open air missing his face. "Don't touch me!"

He caught my arms and crisscrossed them tightly around my chest, pulling my hands further back in a severe hold. "Ouch, let go!" I jerked my head back hard; dark spots filled my vision as my head connected to his chin with a thud.

"Damn it! You want to know why I'm here, Jinx?" He spat angrily, pulling my arms tighter, speaking in a rushed tone. "Then trust that I'm on your side and I'm here to help you. I'm no traitor. If that isn't enough for you right now, then that's just too damn bad because there is a lot worse of an evil out in this jungle and let me just tell you that *they* aren't here to be your friend. *They* will kill you."

His chest rose and fell in quick short beats. I had never witnessed Ghost so angry, or his implored words edged with candor. I believed him. Damn him. Accepting what he said wasn't easy, but what other option was there?

I swallowed my pride. "If you betray me Ghost, so help me..." I bit off the trailing words because I really wanted to believe he was being honest with me, but seeing him in this forest with that uniformed man did nothing for my confidence in him. He released my arms and I shook them out, swiped up my bag, and began to stride off.

"You're going the wrong way."

I turned around without looking at him, and stalked off in the opposite direction. He muttered something behind me, his deep tone blurring his words together.

If I never stepped foot in a jungle again, I would've been okay with that. The razor-sharp leaves carved lines across my arms and vines threatened decapitation with every shift in direction. Wet ferns saturated my clothes, and spider webs laced my exposed skin. Shivers ran down my arms as I hurriedly brushed them off. The growth thickened the further we walked through the labyrinth. I followed him and kept quiet but the silence was deafening. I couldn't bear it any longer. "How did you find me, Ghost?" I whispered. That one question reeled in my thoughts. I couldn't come up with an explanation that made any sense.

Watching his backside, and the muscles shifting beneath the fitted black shirt as he pushed away at dangling vines, stirred flutters in my stomach. *What is wrong with me?* Being alone with no one to talk to obviously tainted my mind, but not knowing what the hell was going on niggled away at my patience. The nonresponse pissed me off to no end. Compliance wasn't my forte. The flutters took a back seat to my rebellious nature.

"Ghost!"

Stopping mid stride, he twisted around with a glare to match my own. A thick finger went to his lips, "shhh."

I humored him regardless of the fact that I wanted to rip his head off. As he started walking I swooped down, and scooped up a thick chunk of wood, smacking the middle of his back. Bullseye.

He whipped around and glared at me. What little light shone through the wild branches was enough to capture the narrowed eyes and tight angry lips. I could even see a vein pulsing on the side of his neck and I tipped him a false smile.

He stepped over a log, pushing away from a fallen branch with heavy determined steps and stood a few paces away. Sweat glistened across his forehead. He leaned toward me. "Do you want me to change my mind? Do you want to be here all alone? Because if you keep pushing me Jinx, I swear I will turn around right now..." he stopped himself, wiping a hand across his brow. He closed the gap, lowering his voice "Jinx," he said softly, shaking his head. "I know you don't understand any of this," his arms circled around in the air, "and I plan on telling you everything, but trust me when I tell you we need to get out of here. There is a boat waiting for us off Terrapin's hook and if we don't make it back in time, it will leave and we will be stranded here. I am asking you—begging you to trust what I am saying is the truth." His pleading eyes searched mine.

I fidgeted with the jumpsuit circling my waist and looked up at him through narrowed eyes. My arms crossed against my chest. "What is Terrapin, Ghost?"

He released a heavy breath. "Terrapin is an island in the Rouche. It's not located on the traditional Nordic maps. As far as I know, it's off government radar. I don't quite understand it myself, but it's paramount we reach the boat before sunrise.

Trust me, it's our only chance of getting off this island."

I cringed at the thought of staying another day. He abandoned his post regardless what it would cost him, knowing he could not return without a harsh punishment, for one thing. Me. "I'm sorry I threw the stick at you." I looked down. "You're only trying to help, and I know you want me to believe that. I want to believe that. But you have to understand where I'm coming from. I will kill you with my bare hands if you're lying to me, Ghost. Trust *that*." My voice shook with emotion. "There's a boat we need to catch. Lead the way." I tightened the flight suit around my waist, and adjusted my hold on the small knapsack. He gazed at me, and after a moment he turned and led us onward. The question was, could I trust Ghost, and if so, how far?

EIGHT

Salty air filled my lungs and stung my nose. My eyes watered, clouding my vision. I squinted and caught sight of a silvery glimmer off the coast. A rounded metallic object rode along the pulse of the waves as they came crashing into the rocky shore.

A harsh sneeze erupted. Ghost turned a curious eye toward me. "Keep it down," he whispered. I brushed a hand across my nose and sniffled.

"I think I'm allergic to you."

A sudden jerk, hard on my arm, pulled me back with spine-snapping force. I stumbled at the unexpected pull, my fingers grazing small sharp rocks lining the edge between the beach and the jungle as I caught my footing. "What the…" His hand shot up, silencing me…again. I was getting tired of him shushing me. He jabbed a finger to the left. I snuck a glance around his bulky shoulders down the shoreline to find a small group of figures walking along the beach, barely close enough to make out among the shadows dancing off the reflective waves from the moon's light.

My chest constricted. *Could it be the soldiers looking for me?* I shot Ghost a worried glance and settled back on my haunches running my hands through my tangled hair. We had to make it to the boat, but how could we streak across the sand unseen? I looked up at Ghost as if he could read the endless questions rolling through my mind, hoping he had a plan.

We could hear the voices over the crashing waves below. They were getting closer. And there were more of them than I thought. With his brows pinched tight, Ghost pulled a small pen-like device from his pocket. A faint yellowish light blinked on and off as he aimed it toward the boat. A yellow flash mimicked back from the water and a few seconds later, the boat slowly descended below the water's surface, disappearing from sight. A lump formed in my throat. I wanted to reach out to the boat. I wanted to make a run for it. Anything was better than watching it slip back into the murky darkness of the Rouche. He pulled the back of my sweat-drenched tank top, and I pushed to my feet, retreating into the dark folds of the jungle.

"Damn. On to plan B."

"Wait? What? And, what plan B? Ghost, please tell me that boat is coming back. Tell me we aren't stuck on this island. I need to get out of here. We could outrun them! We could make it. I know we could. We can wait for them to pass and make a run for it!" I tried to convince him with pleading eyes as much as convincing myself. My heart pounded in rapid succession. There was no chance of making it down the rocky slope, over the beach and to the boat that had already retreated. He tore his eyes from mine and looked down, and my gaze trailed his. Black t-shirt material was clenched tightly around my fingers. My heart skipped a beat. I hadn't realized what I had done, I threw back Ghost's shirtsleeve like a virus. "Sorry."

"We can't risk the boat being seen. We should get out of here before they get too close and you give us away."

"What's that supposed to mean?" I hissed quietly, snatching up a broken twig, hurling it across the gnarled path, and muttered under my breath. He could be such a jackass!

"Nothing. Never mind."

I sighed. I had a million questions and nobody to ask. I was thick in the middle of a jungle with a guy who guarded secrets as easily and as naturally as breathing. He leapt over a fallen limb, and I wondered what I really knew about him. It wasn't much.

We slid back into the obnoxious jungle. Deep revulsion to this never ending cycle began taking its toll. My eyelids dropped heavily, bobbing up and down, worn from the anxiety and the ache of defeat.

"Ghost, I need to stop for minute. I don't think I can move another step." Leaning forward, hands on knees, my head dropped lifelessly. Sleepiness was hard to fight when the air hung thick with humidity and pressed against every dip of my eyes and every inhale and exhale I took. He had no idea what I had been through and he sure as hell wasn't showing any consideration as he hustled through the vines like a slithering snake.

He slid smoothly over and around large stones and trees with ease, making the task seem effortless, as if he knew every curve and fissure on the island. He hadn't weathered a plane crash, or escaped imprisonment. He hadn't had to trudge through a never ending jungle filled with mysterious creatures and no explanation of where this *hell* actually was. Well, until today.

"You gonna be alright, Jinx?" His hand rested hesitantly on my shoulder. I envisioned what I must have looked like. Mangled hair, angry red scratches all over my body, dark circles below my eyes, and chapped lips from near dehydration, which was evidently toying with my logical thinking because I actually convinced myself I was glad Ghost was there…with me.

I waited a moment before I replied. It felt good to embrace the numbness and silence, but going through everything that happened, a myriad of emotions. My head tilted up, and my eyes narrowed.

"I haven't been alright since my jet was shot down by Rucky…"

His lips parted and eyes widened.

"I haven't been alright since I witnessed you conversing with the uniformed guard and I haven't been alright since the boat lowered into the water, abandoning us." I stepped so close our bodies nearly touched and looked straight into the depth of his dark eyes. "So if you want to know if I am alright—no, Ghost. I am not *alright*." A salty tear slithered down my cheek.

"Shit. I'm sorry, Jinx." He ran a hand over the back of his neck, looking off to the side, obviously rocked by my confession. "I understand why you haven't trusted me," he said. His hand swept up, and a finger brushed away the lone tear on my face.

A moment passed and I stepped back unsure how to handle the strange vibe coursing through my veins. He took my hand. Holding it tight, he pulled me forward and our bodies nearly collided. My chest heaved with emotion. A warm callused hand tipped up my chin so that I was forced to look into those velvety brown eyes. There was an unsettling expression on his face—the one he always got before telling me something he knew I'd hate. Something passed behind his eyes. He dropped his hand and stepped back. I was left standing there frozen, unsure if I had lost my mind completely.

He cleared his throat. "We...uh, we should probably keep moving. You're the toughest woman I know, you can make it a little longer, right?"

I spun around lazily, and walked away. Of course I was tough. But the thorns of a rose only protected the surface. It wasn't the physical that affected my tough exterior, it was the mental that tugged and pulled down the structure supporting it. I was delusional if I thought Ghost was something other than self-righteous, but I saw *something* pass in his eyes. *What's running through that head of yours, Ghost?*

I lost all sense of time as we continued our trek through Terrapin. The nights were drawn out longer, days shorter. I couldn't decipher which way was which. My legs burned like a thousand suns, were tight and threatening to lock up. The landscape escalated and the ground rose with every burning step. I couldn't hear Ghost, though I knew he was there, close behind. The terrain began transforming from dirt and vines to moss covered rock. The vegetation didn't seem quite as thick. Sweat outlined my face, and my tank top was soaked through. My boot slipped off a slippery rock, tossing me against the uneven ground with a thud.

Pain burst from my knee. "Damn, that hurt."

"Hey, are you okay? We can take a rest here. But we need to find somewhere to camp for the night."

I turned, sitting on a moss-cushioned flat rock. My arms felt heavy and my legs curled in. I dropped my head in my hands, closing my eyes. The lack of feeling overtook me. Ghost settled beside me. Before I knew what was happening, he put an arm around my shoulders and pulled me close to his side. I didn't resist. I couldn't. What was this kindness? My head rested on my bony knees, hiding the tears escaping.

"Everything will be alright in your world again, Jinx. I promise you. We will find out who's behind this treachery," he whispered and sweetly drew comforting circles across my back.

For several disoriented seconds, I couldn't remember where I was. I pushed up from the flat rock and stretched my legs, yawning. I flinched. My foul morning breath jarred me awake. "I'd kill for a tube of toothpaste and a toothbrush. How long was I out?" I said, trying to conceal the stench with my hand.

Ghost handed over a cupped leaf filled with swirls of pinks and deep purple hued liquid. The colors appeared opulent and smelled of ripened berries. Terrapin was full of odd surprises.

"Go ahead. Drink it."

I turned a questioning eye toward Ghost. "What is this?" I asked, tilting the leaf back and forth, watching the pearlescent colors shimmer and swirl.

Ghost leaned back against a tree and hiked up his knee with a half-moon smile. "I mixed a packet of vitamin enhancer with water and vine berries. They must be a disingenuous fruit on the island. But I've seen them at the Trifecta Farmer's Market." He ran a hand across his forehead.

Throughout the year, Gowen, Senna, Prave, Lucia, and Nordic came together to sell and trade produce and goods. Not only was it a show of good relations between the five countries, it gave the opportunity for people to come together in good faith, sample and purchase rarities from the other countries' shops. I snuck a glance. Ghost zoned in on the leaf cupped between my hands, as if he was another island away, deep in thought.

"Why did you do it? Why would you risk your pilot status—your life—for me? Is this some desperate attempt to win my heart over, be the hero who saves me? You never did answer my question, Ghost."

His gaze remained fixed on the leaf. He cleared his throat. "Remember that morning on Senders Rock? The morning I told you Advisor Turner sent the comm about reporting earlier to the Air Field?" He pulled his eyes to mine. Those deep brown eyes were captivating in their own right. There shouldn't be such long lashes and pleasing eyes on a guy. Ever. They were panty droppers, trouble starters, and provoked recreational activities I wanted no part of.

I chewed my bottom lip, looking back to the swirling liquid. "You pissed me off that day. Of course I remember," I said a bit too harshly.

"Jinx," he said, contemplating his choice of words. "There's been some shady stuff going on. I had reason to believe you were a target, so I'd kept an eye on you."

I turned an evil glare his way. His hands shot up in defense. "I had to! Listen to me. I've been working under Advisor Sweet and Turner for over a year. After one of my shifts, I went home and failed to realize I left the Simulator scheduling file in Turners' office. And since the schedule was due the next morning, I went back to get it. When I returned to Turner's office to extract the folder from the cabinet, there were a few odd files I hadn't remembered ever seeing before."

A coppery taste coated my tongue. My leg bounced in quick succession. "You said you believed I was in danger…We both know Rucky was involved, but who else? And you were stalking me? I knew you were off, but following someone around isn't okay, it's creepy." My voice amped up.

Ghost's hands shot up into the air. "Whoa, settle down, let me finish. Just let me explain, please," he pleaded. "I pulled one of the files out; no one was in the office. That file contained a list of names, Jinx. Names of pilots who have either disappeared or…" He looked away and pinched the bridge between his eyes.

"It was a hit-list, Jinx. I swear with everything in me. A list of names—targets." He rubbed the back of his neck, clearly affected by what he had uncovered.

"And?" I said, waiting for more. It was written all over his expression, there was something else eating away at his composure.

"And your name was on that list as well as others that went missing about eight months ago."

My breath hitched. Visions of friends, comrades, and pilots who had vanished, crashed—lives taken, for what? Why would someone target pilots and why was *I* on that list? Someone wanted me dead. But why? My chest constricted, and I pressed my eyes shut. He said something but I couldn't even hear him. I became disoriented, and pissed, and...and...oh God.

"Calm down...breathe, Jinx." He was by my side in a blink. I couldn't think. I sat there without feeling or emotion. "What else was on there? Why was my name on there, Ghost? There had to be something," I wheezed between gulping air. He put his arm around me and drew soothing circles against my back. How many times had he touched me now?

But I didn't want his comfort, I wanted answers. Pushing away the fear, confusion, and worry, I chose to exercise everything that punctured a hole in my heart to feed my anger, to listen intently and absorb what he had to say. Knowledge would keep me alive.

"I can't answer that question. But there is more." Shifting his weight, his black boots shot out past my oversized borrowed ones.

"I didn't get a chance to look through the whole file. I heard footsteps coming down the hall, so I took the schedule and shoved the file back, but a handwritten label on the folder stood out. Terrapin. At the time, it didn't make any sense. Something just *felt* wrong. I didn't know what Terrapin was or meant, but when I saw the list of names, and some of those names scratched off...I began to wonder. I recognized the name Albatross. Do you remember him? He was the night shift janitor who went missing last year. Then farther down on the list I came across your name."

"I remember him. His name was Donnie, but the students called him by his last name. He slinked around the halls, pale as a ghost pushing the squeaky mop bucket down the halls. Why didn't you tell anyone? This all could have been stopped," I said, twisting to look up at Ghost.

"As soon as I got back to the complex, I did some research. It was a complete dead-end. It was as if Terrapin didn't exist. If Nordic techies traced my search, and if Commander DeMarco or his Advisors were hiding Terrapin, no doubt they would detain me. Trusting anyone with that sort of information would make me subject of defying the government. Not only that, but I didn't have a lead as to who he was working with. It could've been anyone. So, I took extra precautions, recruited a few extra eyes and ears to help me out."

"Oh no, Ghost, what did you do?"

He leaned back on his arms and crossed his ankles. "I enlisted a few of my most trusted friends to help."

He must have had faith in those *friends*. If anyone had

caught wind of what he was up to, he wouldn't have made it to Terrapin. I didn't want to imagine the cruelty that would have been bestowed upon him had he been caught. A shudder raced down my body. I took a sip of the cool liquid and briefly closed my eyes as the savory juice coated my tongue. A burst of refreshing liquid splashed around in my mouth.

"Karrie is assigned in Land Resources building which is strategically placed next to the special ops offices. I knew she had some access to maps and locations, so we met up."

I rolled my eyes. Of course he asked his most *trusted* friends. They were his groupies, his recreational activities. No one else would risk getting caught doing Ghost's dirty work... unless they had a vested interest. It was a no-brainer. He had them wrapped around his little finger, do just about anything he asked. I stopped myself before my mouth spilled unladylike retorts. Why should I care if he manipulated those brainless twits? He was using them. So why had it bothered me?

"Then I assume you found the island on a map?" The suns' rays highlighted thin golden streaks through his brown, sweat-spiked hair and glimmered off the golden tips of his eyelashes.

"No," he said. "There wasn't a trace of the island's existence anywhere to be found, which didn't make sense. Either they really don't know about Terrapin, or they just are really good at keeping it to themselves...or a select few."

"So how did you find me? You're telling me you kept getting dead-ends, but not how you actually knew where I was. If you weren't able to locate Terrapin on any maps, how did you end up here?"

His lashes fluttered and I turned away busying myself with the flight-suit arms tied around my waist. "Don't flip out," he said in an almost pleading tone. "I..." he cleared his throat. "I chipped your comm."

Aw, shit. No he did not just say he put a tracking chip inside my comm. "You were spying on me?" I whirled around, shaking my head in disbelief. Juice spilled, soaking through my leggings. My heart rate accelerated to unnatural speeds. The inner animal couldn't be reined in. Ghost admitted to invading my privacy. Without any indication, or even how he managed to do it, he succeeded. It was unnerving. Scary as hell. What else had he been hiding from me? I needed to calm down, breathe, and collect myself before my trembling hands choked him. "Maybe if you had bothered to tell me the truth in the first place, we wouldn't be stranded here together! This disaster would have been avoided."

He walked away, raking his fingers through his hair. "I did try to warn you but you wouldn't listen. You're so stubborn sometimes."

"So I've been told," I said with a cold smile. I thought back to the morning before my last flight, the attempts he made and I shot him down without question. What he didn't realize was that it was already too late. The plan was set in motion. But, he did try, and that counted for something. "Under the circumstances I understand why you did it, but I'm still pissed. *Very* pissed, actually. Where's your comm? I want it. I'm getting out of here."

"I don't have it," he said. "After your jet went down, I

disposed of mine." His lips tipped up into a half smile. "Actually, it's on a floating sonar detector a mile off land in the Rouche. But Jinx," he continued. "There's one more thing you need to know. When I opened up your comm to place the chip inside, there was another one in it. Someone had already been tracking you." I drew in a breath, and covered my heart in shock.

"I'm not trying to be anyone's hero," he said. "I did what I felt was the right thing to do. Because I've learned that some things in life are worth the risk. And besides, I'm still determined to get that dinner."

NINE

I was still slightly pissed at the fact that Ghost chipped my communication device, but after I simmered down and walked about five miles, I finally was able to think rationally and decided I wouldn't practice torture techniques on him, even though the temptation was strong. There were two sides to my conscience, the red and the white—the white being sensible and thought things through, and the red, well, the red was the complete opposite. Most of my life, red dominated.

I had come around slowly by his standards, so he said. And of course I argued and held out a little longer just to prove my point. We walked in silence and it was torture. I had enough silence for the past...however long I had been on Terrapin. Forgiveness did not come easy, but being as we were the only two people from Nordic, and Ghost the only one I knew, I sucked it up and pulled up my big-girl stretch pants. In reality, had he not acted, I would have been roaming around all alone. My heart sunk at the thought.

The old cabin looked worse than I had remembered. The wooden porch drooped from rot and ruin. The door, kicked from its hinges, laid in pieces littered around the entry. Ghost walked passed me, and ducked inside the cabin as if he owned the place.

"Did you even consider someone could be hiding in there?" I mean, with my track record I wouldn't have busted in without checking the place out. I heard him mumble something about being *paranoid*. Of course I was!

He slung his bag onto the bed and stripped off his holster, his back to me.

"There'd be fresh tracks or even a truck if someone was. Do you remember how far you traveled to get here?" he asked, digging through his bag.

I wanted to thump the back of his head with an iron thumb. "No," was all I said. I pulled one of the chairs over and sat down, relief poured from my limbs as I slouched lazily onto it.

"Let's walk the perimeter. You go around that way, and I'll go around this way," he instructed. "We'll meet up back here by the porch."

He rifled through his bag and tucked a knife inside his waistband. With a huff, I agreed. It wasn't like the place was a mansion. I was pretty confident he could manage on his own, but I played along and did as he asked.

The perimeter check was uneventful until I heard a grunt emanating from the opposite side of the cabin. I tore around the corner in a sprint to find him prying a nailed down board from the shacks back corner.

"I heard your struggle and it scared the hell out of me! What are you doing?" I asked warily.

His muscles strained as he tore away a portion of the board. It slipped from his grasp and sailed through the air. I ducked quickly, avoiding decapitation. A dark hole opened up as Ghost peeled away a few more planks.

"This," he said as he ducked down, stepping into the space, and swallowed by the darkness.

"What's in there? Be careful. There could be a trap or snakes." Tingles danced through my body. I hated snakes and they were the one creature I would run away from screaming. I took a precautionary step back, then another.

His back inched out, dipping beneath the opening. I couldn't help noticing his tight round ass. The way his pants hung low on his hips stirred flutters in my stomach. He backed out, pulling behind him an old motorbike.

My eyes shot wide. "Nice work, but how did you know that was in there?" I asked with excitement, pointing at the broken wall. I hurried over and ran my fingers over the dust covered vinyl seat, leaving trail marks along the way. I couldn't tell what shape the bike was in under the years of filth that concealed every surface, but the wheels were intact, and the mechanical parts all appeared present.

"There was a small latch at the bottom, and the base is made of wood. Notice it isn't raised like the rest of the cabin? Plus..." he pointed to a torn 4x4, "the lumber is different, fresher."

I had not remembered the addition, but under the circumstances, my focus was on the men ransacking the place. I squatted beside the front tire, pulling at a chain circling the rubber tube. "Why would someone put chains on tires?" I looked up to him with questioning eyes.

"Who knows?" He shrugged.

Ghost began wiping off the brownish powder. "I'll have to pull it apart and clean it before I can get it working." He circled the bike, tinkering with a rubber tube. It looks like it's been around for a while." His lips arched at the corner into a wide smile.

"What's that grin for?" I asked, mood lifting.

"Can't I be excited? Man project," he said, giddily, rubbing his hands together.

My hopes had heightened with the newfound bike and Ghost's eagerness. An ache in my chest formed with thoughts of my beloved motorcycle in Nordic. I released a heavy breath and smiled. I saved my measly earnings for years to buy my motorcycle. It was the only possession I truly owned of any value other than a tiny locket given to me as I left the orphanage. I remembered the matron handing over the cloth bag, confused, and wondering what was inside. She explained that when Matron Larue brought me inside, she found the trinket tied around my infant wrist. In Nordic, if you were in the Academy, wages were poor.

Commander DeMarco micromanaged everything, even down to the toilet paper rations.

It took hours to clean up the old silver bike. I was amazed

at how well preserved it appeared, besides the normal wear and tear, it cleaned up nicely. Ghost and I pulled the bike apart bit by bit, and blew out the carburetor. He tossed a few jokes around and told me his mission was to make me crack a smile. And because he said that, I made an extra effort to hold out as long as I possibly could.

Thankfully, the previous owners were kind enough to leave unused and partly full cans of oil and gas in the hideaway. Ghost filled the gas tank and I placed the empty container inside the hidey-hole, but quickly, afraid a snake would then take advantage and slither out. We both stepped back, admiring our work. His elbow brushed mine as he shifted his weight.

"Hold still," he said.

I froze. My thoughts instantly drew a large coiling snake at my feet, but then a gentle wipe of his thumb swept across my cheek. I jerked away in response. "What are you doing?" I covered his path with my hand, as if the man-germs burned me.

"Hold still. You made it worse. And don't look at me like I'm your favorite dessert, it's not helping the situation any."

There was a tease in his tone. "What situation?" I asked. "And I'm not. Trust me." I displayed the most repulsed expression I could. The hem of his shirt pulled up over his crossed arms and cleared his head. "Whoa." My palms flew up. "You're reading the signs all wrong. Put your shirt back on," I pleaded to him. My eyes widened, soaking up the definition of his stomach. *Holy abs.*

"You like what you see?" He laughed, waggling his eyebrows.

I gained my composure and mocked a laugh. "I was just

thinking you're almost as toned as I am. Close, but not quite there yet, big guy," I said, patting his stomach.

His closed lipped dimpled smile awakened something inside of me. The same smile I saw the morning on Senders Rock, the one that sent tingles through my body. I wanted to pull my eyes away. But he was beautiful." I wondered how many women have kissed those pouty lips.

"Now hold still. I'm not trying to seduce you...yet." He laughed.

"It's hard to take you serious when your dimple mocks you." He brought his shirt up to my cheek, gently brushing it across the skin in slow careful circles. The other rested on my shoulder. The closeness of our bodies and the gentleness of his touch warmed my insides. I looked up, watching him concentrate, studying every detail, memorizing every line.

"There you go," he whispered, locking eyes.

The sun sank and the wind picked up. Leaves blew through the broken window and limbs scraped across the metal roof. Ghost stood by the small wood stove, careful to use only dried dead wood. The greener sticks would produce more smoke and possibly bring unwanted attention. As he stood by the stove, I couldn't make my eyes look away. I tried hating him. I truly did.

He warmed up two compressed military meals and sat down beside me. His leg rested against mine as we leaned back against the bed's frame. We sat silently and dug into the food. Normally I would bitch about the MRE's, but I hadn't had a full meal since I left Nordic and this was amazing even for a military meal. Steam rose from the stewed beef and vegetables, fanning my face.

"Tomorrow at first light we'll head out and look for the camp. Now that we have the bike, we can cover more ground in less time. Are you sure you don't remember anything that would help us locate it—a building, a land formation…anything?"

I shook my head. "No. It was too dark. The fog was thick and…" All I could see was the dark of night and the smell of a dwindling fire. "There's nothing, Ghost. Like I said before, it must be on lower terrain. I swore I climbed a steep, wooded incline. Other than that, I have nothing."

I yawned and stretched out my arms. "What are we going to do if we find it? We don't have a plan. Walking in blindly will get us killed, and honestly, I don't want to find it, Ghost. There's just too much uncertainty right now. Maybe we should focus on getting back to Nordic." I took the last bite and set down the plate.

"You're not going to like what I'm about to say, but think about this before you say anything, okay?" He glanced at me, and I nodded. "I know you want to go back to Nordic. You feel a sense of duty to the country, to your comrades. But how can you be certain any one of them isn't involved in this, too? When we learned your four-ship went down, it was disregarded and said to be an 'unexpected accident,' and is being looked into. We can't trust anyone there, Jinx. No one."

I considered what he said. It was true. I had been determined to go back to the very place that had more secrets than Terrapin. "So what do you propose we do? Where will we go?" Thoughts flooded my mind. *Where were we going to go?*

"For now, we stay here. Look for the camp, dig for information."

"Honestly, how long do you plan on staying here? Those men could come back at any time. Is this how our lives will be? On the run until eventually they catch up and then what? There isn't a soul on this island going to help us. Were alone, and being hunted."

We cleared away debris, setting the table and chairs off to the side beneath the window, brushed the broken glass in a corner and shook out the dusty sheet from the end of the bed. There wasn't much space in the cabin, and the mattress was in no shape to sleep on, so Ghost laid the sheet across the floor. It made sense we would sleep side-by-side—the floor was only so big, and the furniture took up space—but it was a little awkward.

I unlaced my boots and tossed them on the lumpy mattress. Ghost pulled his shirt up, clearing his head, and shoved it inside his bag. He turned his head and we stood there, our eyes locked on one another. Warmth enveloped me. Every muscle in my body tightened—first from perplexity and then from something else. The moment felt intimate; time stood still. Tonight was different from the last. I fell asleep from exhaustion. This was the first time I would sleep beside a man willingly, and oddly enough, I was okay with that.

"I'll take this side," I said. And in the matter of milliseconds, I was curled up on my side, my arm tucked beneath my head.

Ghost settled beside me on his back, using his arms as pillows. He glanced my way, a faint, gloating smile crossing his face.

"What?" I asked.

"I got my dinner." I shoved his arm playfully and couldn't help but laugh. He had me there. I wasn't fully comfortable knowing there were men roaming the jungle with guns, but with Ghost curled up beside me, I was able to let my mind go and fall asleep.

A movement woke me. I peeled a heavy eye open. Ghost's body is molded to my back, heated breaths tickling my neck, and a heavy arm draped across my midriff. Too tired to smile, I closed my eye and fell back to sleep wrapped in Ghosts's warmth.

TEN

Traces of morning light danced across my eyelids. I groaned, rolled over and wiped away the sleep from my eyes. A path of sunlight shone through the open doorway. Ghost was there in silhouette; his shirtless back leaned against the rim of the opening deep in thought.

I remembered the dreaded 'morning after' conversations with the ladies. The locker room and Hangers bar was a classroom of sorts. Now I knew what they meant about the morning after, even though Ghost and I hadn't done anything other than sleep beside each other. There was an intimacy in the way he curled up behind me, having his arm draped over my waist. For once, my guard was down, and I wasn't afraid my innocence was threatened. But I'd always harbor a sense of regret befriending a boy before he'd attempted to rip it away.

"How long have you been up?" I asked, stretching my arms

to the sky. I smoothed my rumpled tank top and shuffled to the opening.

"Good morning." His voice was monotone as if he was somewhere else, staring out into nothingness. "I've been up on and off throughout the night," he said, sneaking a glance my way then back to the jungle. Dark stubble curved around his jawline, blending seamlessly into his wavy hairline.

"There's a storm moving in. There's enough fuel to get around for a while, but it won't last forever. The sooner we find the campsite, the better."

I shook my head. I was in awe of him. He was in complete control and so at home in this place. I couldn't imagine what I would be doing or where I would be if he had not shown up.

"I'm glad you're here," I said.

He whipped his head around. I almost flinched as his steady gaze traveled down my face to my lips, and even though I knew to shield my heart, it pulsed with warmth. My lips parted. He leaned closer.

I gasped as a sharp, piercing pain shot through my foot. I peered down at a small pool of crimson circling my heel. Large warm hands lifted my foot and quickly pulled away at the penetrated shard of glass. My arms braced the wall as Ghost held up the sliver prism into the dimming light. It was thin, long and sharp.

With a shaky breath I said, "Thank you, but you didn't have to do that." He flicked it into the waxy green growth. The moment between us had dissolved too quickly.

I packed up our bags while Ghost moved the bike around

to the front. The dirt-bike was aged with rusted pipes, a torn pleather seat and beat-up handlebars. I couldn't help but notice a circular black device cupped over the exhaust. It stood out as it looked shiny and new compared to the abandoned, weathered bike.

"What's that?" I asked pointing to the object.

He looked up from behind the seat. His eyes were smiling. "Silencer." Then his head disappeared again, busy at work.

I had to give credit where credit was due, but who carries around a silencer? "Ghost, explain to me why you brought this instead of a phone. There are like, a million…," my arms circled the air, "a million other things I can think of that would be far more useful than a silencer."

His head popped up at an angle. His eyes pinched inward. "I *did* bring a cell," he huffed. "It doesn't work here. Technology doesn't work here." He emphasized the word 'technology' as if disgusted.

I mulled over what he said. *Technology doesn't work here.* "That's absurd," I stated. "Everyone has it. Even Prave has it, and that island isn't big enough to spit on." It was ridiculous, really, the thought of it. *Wait.* "How do you know?" Was it because the towers were too far? Nordic had impressive technology. I couldn't wrap my mind around the idea of having zero contact with the outside world. Who would live like that?

"It's ready," Ghost said, wiping his hands down the black cargo pants like they were caked in mud, ignoring my question.

I swung my leg over the back of the bike without hesitation, wrapping my arms firmly around his waist, warmth seeped through the material separating us. I tried to retrace the journey from the camp to the shack best I could, but everything looked the same—the same trees with long jagged palms, the vines with curling tendrils wrapping around and streaming from tree to tree. Their colors were vibrant and warm; almost comforting.

I made the sign of our Holy Mother, and we sputtered forward weaving around the vegetation toward the very place I said I would never go back to.

Plumes of dust blew across the path as the motorcycle whirled to a stop just inside the jungles beveled edge, overlooking a camp. Had we found it? The cliff was Terrapin's very own Senders Rock and I missed my morning rides and the deep rumble when I revved the engine. The mechanical silencer was a blessing, silencing the growl of the motorbike. I unwrapped myself from Ghost's waist as he killed the switch, and locked the breaks. Being pressed against Ghost was playing hell on my self-control. I swung my leg around, stepping away, and crept closer to the ledge in a low crouch.

I spotted the Machiavellian band of followers stockpiling various weapons onto a cargo trailer hitched to a rusty military style truck. Men milled around the campsite sporting dark green cargo pants, the same black t-shirt with military style boots performing various tasks among the littered buildings and camouflaged tents. It was a brilliant location strategically. The cliff-like wall provided a shield against the westerly winds. The presence of luxuriant vegetation concealed rock fissures supplying fresh water. Large tropical trees and plants circled to the southeast border that butted up against the northeast line of lofty hills separating north from south.

My eyes pinched, as I strained to examine the camp. I wanted a closer look. Ghost crept up beside me. "Here, use these," he said in a low whisper, offering a compact pair of binoculars as if he read my thoughts. I looked away biting my lip and hating myself for the feelings I kept pushing down.

"Thank you." His fingers brushed against mine in the exchange. My heart sputtered from the contact. I didn't dare a peek. Only a few feet separated us.

Clinking of metal hissed through the air. I pressed the small lenses to my eyes and, swiveled to my left seeking out the source. Off to the far side of the structures stood a group of shirtless men slashing away with precision as they hammered at the stone base of the mountainside.

"They're chipping away at stone, Ghost." I lifted the binoculars away from my eyes, exhaling a deep breath. I wondered what they were up to, and why they were hacking away the stone. What was their agenda? Terrapin was a mystery within itself, but there had to be more to the island and those unprincipled, debauched men.

I sunk back down onto the ground, wrapping my arms around my knees. "If Advisor Turner is involved…" I chewed the dried, cracked skin on my lower lip. "If he truly is, Ghost, how do we know if he's working with others in Nordic? How do we know if we can truly depend on or trust anyone?"

We sat overlooking the camp below, both lost in deep thoughts. The sky drew its own kind of darkness against the ominous feeling I got from the camp. The wind strengthened.

Currents of spiraling particles and debris whipped at our exposed hands and faces.

Ghost broke the silence. "Is this where you were held?" he asked.

"I don't know," I said, shaking my head as if clarity would strike and every detail would surface. "I'm going over the details from that night. I remember a wooden door, and I tumbled from a raised building to the ground." I looked down at my fingers. "I remember crawling through dirt and leaves. There was an incline—pretty steep if I recall. My arms burned and my feet ached, but I know it wasn't stone I climbed up. I don't know."

Ghost squeezed my hand and released it. "We will keep an eye on this location—figure out what they're up to, and more importantly, who they are. There could be another camp somewhere we haven't found yet. Let's head back to the cabin and look again tomorrow."

Large drops of water sporadically littered the ground; I looked down at the nut sized droplet. "Let's get out of here."

ELEVEN

The rain poured down relentlessly. I was soaked, and my clothes were clung to my skin like a wetsuit. I repositioned myself, tightening my arms around Ghost's waist as the bike bounced over small mounds and dipped into oversized divots. Pools of muddy water shot up from holes, and coated us with grime and filth. I squeezed my eyes closed, lips in a firm line, anticipating the next wave of dirty brown water to come spraying up.

The silencer worked like a charm. The loud rumble of the bike was no more than a kitten's purr now the silencer was attached. He was like a magician holding all the secret tricks, only to unveil them at the right time. With the darkened sky and the murky waters flooding the terrain, I wondered how we would ever make it back to the cabin without growing a set of fins.

A muffled sound emanated from Ghost. His arm shot out, swinging behind my back and, holding me in place. The bike took a nasty dip and the front wheel popped up. A loud crack shook our bodies and sparks of bright fire launched toward us in ribbons. I screamed and ducked behind him, making myself as small as I could. Ghost accelerated, and leaned to the left as a tree limb crashed down on the ground. It punched into the forest floor, tossing debris and chips of wood in every direction. How had he been able to see where he was going? It was virtually impossible to my eyes.

Finally, we pulled up to the cabin. We sprinted from the bike and sprang for cover, barreling into the cabin like a herd of cattle. I flung my hands, flicking water to the floor.

Suddenly, a light lit up the dark room. Ghost placed a flashlight up on end, casting a faint circular glow around the ceiling and walls.

"You packed a flashlight," I said reverently. "What didn't you bring, Ghost?" I twisted the bottom of my sopping tank-top between my fingers. Water trickled to the floor. When I looked back up, Ghost had stripped away his shirt. His bare back greeted me as he dug into his backpack. Black cargo pants hung low on his waist and I followed the dip and curves of his muscles down the arch to his waistline. Drops of water slid down his smooth tanned skin.

I cleared my throat. "I don't suppose you brought me a change of clothes, right? I mean, you brought everything else." I laughed awkwardly, keenly aware of my tattered attire and ripe smell. I just wanted to leave this island, get back to my life, and figure out who the rebels were.

With his back to me he said, "I've got an extra shirt you can wear until yours dries, or you can walk around naked."

Right. Like that was going to happen. "I'm not going anywhere near you naked," I murmured when I drew my eyes away. My heart skipped a beat. "I want to leave early. I'm not missing the boat a second time."

Truthfully, I didn't think we'd find the camp where I was held before the boat came for us again. And now that Ghost was there, I grew comfortable with him being around. The prospect of being stranded on the island wasn't what I feared anymore.

"Hello, friend."

My head snapped around. A busty brunette leaned against the door frame, arms crossed. My body took a defensive stance. "Who are you?" My voice was soft and lethal; it sent chills down my spine. Ghost's bag slipped from his fingers and hit the floor with a loud *thunk*. He faced the woman across from me. The color drained from his face.

"Pria," Ghost rasped.

Ghost recognized this smug-faced broad. *But, how?*

"Well, are you just going to stand there and stare, or are you going to give an old friend a hug?" The woman, Pria, crossed her arms under her breasts, allowing her shirt to reveal a little more of her. She thrummed her long slender fingers against her biceps. The glow of the flashlight illuminated the space around the room, highlighting her high cheekbones and snake skin outfit that hugged every curve of her body.

Her smile held secrets. And to my dismay, Ghost did, too. If

Ghost noticed the view Pria offered, he was too polite to stare. He ran his hand down the back of his neck. A simple gesture, but I knew Ghost, and I knew him well enough to know that he was anything but happy to see her.

"Mmm," she moaned, edging up to him as if I didn't exist. "I missed your hugs," she crooned, splaying her painted nails against his bare skin. She arched back, gamed his eyes with hers. "Among other things."

My stomach lurched. *Who was she?*

Ghost pulled away, wiping a hand down his face. He glanced over at me with apologetic eyes. My eyes pinched, I had had enough of this reunion.

"Hey!" I shouted. My arms shook. My heart pounded.

"Oh, dear. Why, I didn't see you there." Her voice dripped with smug undertones.

Bullshit. Her false sincerity struck a chord. "G, please introduce me to your little friend?" Her lashes bounced up and down and I held myself back from ripping the jeweled band from her head.

Little friend? She has a nickname for him? "Introductions not necessary." I smiled smugly. "We were just leaving. Right, G?" I wrapped my hand around Ghost's bicep, and pulled him through the doorway and into the trees.

"Slow down, Jinx!"

I spun him around and blasted a glare at him, realizing he was still shirtless. "Who is that, Ghost? Huh?" My pointed finger pounded his chest with each question. My voice raised an octave. "When were you going to tell me the truth? How is it possible you know her—?" I swung my finger toward the door. "—on this island? I'm done with the lies! Quit holding things back from me!"

I didn't need to look back to know Pria stood in the doorway, listening in. I didn't care. What I cared about was his explanation.

"It's not what you think."

"Grow a pair of these—" I palmed his manhood. "—and tell me what you know," I growled, and pulled back.

He folded over, coughed, and pulled up his hand. "Wait."

My leg bounced.

He gave me a sideways glance and mouthed, "Trust me."

I spun on my heel and tore off toward the cabin. My teeth chattered, and my body shook with anger. However, as I swept up my meager belongings, noticing the light glint off the metal knife beside my bag. I raised an eyebrow. The carved initials G.A.D. caught my eye.

I picked the knife up, rolling it over in my hand. My thumb brushed over the carving. Engraved initials like the ones I'd seen by the door, G.D.P.S. Could it be a coincidence or a sick joke? Was this his knife? His cabin? It was all starting to merge together.

"Jinx."

I swallowed a fresh wave of tears, but they still clogged my throat, making it hard to talk without crying.

A warm hand cupped my elbow. I twisted around and faced Ghost. His eyes turned soft, and he lowered his head, brushing his lips to my forehead. I took a deep breath, wanting to pull away. There was always some reason to question others sincerity and motives, to not trust the vultures and liars at my back. I felt empty and weightless.

"I don't want to keep anything from you. But the less you knew about the truth, about me...," he trailed off. "I only wanted to protect you, Jinx. I didn't do this to hurt you. You have to believe me." He looked at me like he was trying to gauge whether or not I believed him. It didn't make a difference.

I stood in silent reverie, and saw the sincerity in his pleading eyes. With a sigh, I set the bag down, and raised the knife. It was like a wedge that spread between Ghost's truth and the reality of the situation. I started to shake, and my eyes grew misty. Ghost only stared at the knife. I wanted him to tell me he had never seen it before. I stood there frozen, my heart pounding, waiting to give him that second chance. But the memories of his words seeped from my veins, and I knew whatever explanation he had to give wouldn't be the truth. *'The less you knew about the truth, about me...'*

"I believed him once." Pria moved in and ran her hand ran over the collar of Ghost's shirt. Ghost regarded me with a look of pity. I felt tired and drained, like there was a gaping hole inside me. And my heart ached.

"What are you talking about?" I asked. Pria's eyes flicked to Ghost, who looked pale and tense. "What is she talking about?" I said more forcefully.

The silence worried me. "I didn't lie to you, Jinx," Ghost said in a soft voice. "But, I didn't tell the entire truth, either."

A flicker of amusement crossed Pria's face. Not only had

she dropped in like a bomb, she was doing her best to piss me off. And nailing it.

"Get on with it. The suspense is killing me," I snapped.

In a breath, Ghost spoke. "Terrapin. This place that doesn't exist to the people of Nordic...is my home."

TWELVE

My vision blurred. The room spun like a tornado. Clarity struck like a fist to my stomach. My heart stuttered as I studied the look crossing Ghost and Pria's face as they shared a quick glance. His confession went straight to the vein. Heat surged down my body, anger boiled the blood running through me, determined to char me from the inside out. Ghost placed a hesitant hand on my shoulder and without thought, my arm cocked back and shot forward connecting with his face. His head jerked back with a grunt and he fell to one knee. His hand swept up to cover his eye.

Pria stepped before me with her palms up. Rage roared like an untamed animal. I punched out with a battle cry, connecting with her cheekbone, and knocked her flat on her ass. Pain exploded through my fist and traveled up my arm.

"Son of a…Damn it," I yelled, cradling my hand to my chest.

"Go burn off some steam, Jinx," Ghost hissed. "Now."

Without a word, I marched from the room and onto the porch, and then ran. I ran until my legs went numb. I ran until I could no longer *feel*. Because feeling hurt. And my heart ached immensely.

I slowed to a hurried walk. Ghost hadn't told me the whole truth, of course; he'd left out the part about being from Terrapin, and how he knew Pria. He had ample opportunity. I believed the lines he fed me, and now I questioned if anything he told me was real or if it was a ploy to earn his trust. How convenient for him. Wasn't he clever...he swooped in like an avenging angel, told me he came for me and to *trust* him. I allowed myself when it was the very thing that I feared. And I was wrong. I clenched my jaw and kept walking. I wouldn't find peace tonight.

The rain had dissipated and the trees obscured the moons glow. With every step, the comm device rubbed the bare skin between my breasts. I missed home. I tried to picture the blue sky, standing on Senders Rock, my little apartment in Nordic. But the images belonged to my past. I felt I was breathing in and out sadness and it was a beautiful release.

The air smelled of muddy, wet earth. My boots swished with each step as my rain soaked socks pressed into the oversized soles, and the sucking sound of thick mud trying to swallow my feet rang in my ears. Slick wet tendrils attached to my neck dripped cool drops down my bare shoulders, and drew prickles across my flesh. I remained silent as the raging war inside slowly dissipated. I wove aimlessly through the jungle trying to make sense of it all. Would I ever understand that guy? I only wanted him to come clean with me. I hadn't asked for too much.

Faint laughter echoed through the night air, barely audible, but enough to raise the hair on my arms. I slowed until I came to a complete stop and listened, tilting an ear in the direction of the sound. I continued forward, creeping toward the source, but I could hear my steps upon the ground as the clunky boots snapped branches and rustled leaves. It was useless to avoid the obstacles. It was too dark in the jungle even with the moon's light that filtered through.

The volume rose and the sky before me lit up like a halo. I maneuvered around bushes and sank behind an outcropping of a snapped tree trunk. Beyond the darkness and a row of trees, a small city built alongside a mountain came to life.

Large bulbous lights strung across the cobbled street, illuminating the buildings lining the strip. The road was void of motor and electric cars, but filled with a throng of people milling about. A man and woman strolled their way through the parting crowd with ease. By their posture and the way they scanned and greeted those they passed, it was obvious they were of importance. The woman was lean and wore clothing similar to what Pria wore—snake skin bodysuit, knee high boots with a low-cut V-neck. A belt loosely wrapped around her waist, but hung slightly low to one side as if weighed down. I ran my hand over the sloppy bun atop my head, noticing the jeweled band around her swept up do, glimmering as it caught the light. His blonde hair pulled and tied at the nape of his neck, brushed the edge of his jacket. They strolled side-by-side, but not close like lovers. Thick shoulders blocked a couple he stopped to talk to.

I wondered who they were and where I was on Terrapin.

Music floated through the air, an entrancing tune, almost hypnotic. It had a hard sensual quality to it which felt unusual to my ears. I had never heard anything like it in Nordic. It was as if they were celebrating something. Maybe they had specialty days as Nordic did. Our biggest celebration was the day we claimed independence from Senna, another bordering country of Nordic.

They appeared so open and *free*. There weren't guards at every turn or Advisors monitoring every action like back home. I scanned over the crowd and the buildings. Homes raised on stilts dotted the outskirts, and I couldn't help but notice lines of clothing strung pole to pole blowing in the breeze. I hesitated in the shadows, trying to decide which direction to go, my next move.

The ground sloped down as I wound my way to a stone stairway. The steep descent would have been a disaster had there not been steps. I slid my palm along the wall for balance, taking one last peek over the edge. All clear. The steps were uneven. Carefully, I turned and tried to climb back, but I couldn't, my legs froze in place. I wasn't a coward and I wasn't in Nordic. Stealing in Nordic resulted in hand amputation. But I had to get out of my filthy clothes and into something clean. Something I would blend into the crowd in. The hair on my neck rose, and shivers danced along my skin. *I'm not in Nordic*, I reminded myself. I took a deep gulp and rushed down the steps. Darted behind the closest house, I slid into the shadows, brushing my hair out of my face. Voices drifted down from the town above, but not a soul walked among them. My heart pounded against my ribs.

After double checking left and right, I shot toward the clothesline, not slowing until I was safely behind a flailing bed sheet, and obscured by the shadows. I tore pants, a shirt, and a fur collard vest from the line blindly. Hunched over, I rushed back to the stairs and up to the safety of the trees.

The clothes were a little loose, but fresh and clean and that was all that mattered. I rolled up the cuffs up and tucked the too long shirt inside the waist of the pants, and slipped the vest on.

"Now, where to put these?" There wasn't time to dig a hole and bury them beneath the dirt. Picking up my soaked clothes, I wadded them into a ball and shoved them behind a tree trunk, covering them beneath a pile of leaves and sticks.

The road into the town was lined with trees and light posts. Ghost said technology didn't work on Terrrapin, but they had electricity in the villages. People of all shapes and sizes, old and young came and went through businesses and doors lining the street. High arched doors and stone-faced storefronts crawled with ivy on both sides. Men, women and children laughed and played games as well as danced to the cheerful tones pulsing through the air. A shoulder bumped into mine. "Sorry." A gruff accented voice said.

I raised my hand and smiled, letting him know it was no bother and took a step, then paused, waiting for a child pulling his mother's arm to follow him. "I have not seen you around before. Are you...?"

"Not interested." I smiled politely, and quickly blended into the crowd. My chest tightened and I wondered if the woman whose clothes I stole would notice her garments on me, or if the man would get the hint. Keeping my head down I angled toward what appeared to be a brew house. Beautiful electric lights illuminated the doorway and a painting of beer mugs hung over the door. I stood in awe at the beautiful colors and noticed they were stones emanating the vivid light.

A strong hand pressed between my shoulder blades and ushered me forward. From the corner of my eye I recognized the man I had dismissed just moments before. We filed down a narrow center aisle between tables and occupied chairs. I wondered what the night would bring and why the man did not take the brushoff. Instead of bolting away, I would use the opportunity to get information about the island, and decided to play along.

He pulled out a chair for me. Instead of sitting, I examined the dark wood and ran my fingers along the glowing inlayed stone at the back's top, the same stones I saw on the sign. The seat was leather. I leaned my palm into it, and then finally sat.

He took the chair beside mine. His shaggy blonde hair looked blue under the glowing stones. Days old stubble trailed around his jawline. A thick cord of leather trailed down into the deep V of his partially unbuttoned shirt. He placed his clasped hands on the table and smiled.

"What's your name?" he asked. His accent was thick and sounded just like Pria's.

Before I could reply, a pretty girl set down two frosted goblets. A dark flash of hair caught my eye. Angling my head to the side, the bar came into view. I swore I'd seen Pria behind the bar, but it was another dark haired gal working quickly taking orders. I brushed the thought aside. No way she could have been there. The waitress poured amber liquid into our goblets, topped off with a thin layer of foam. My stomach growled and my cheeks heated.

"Thank you, but I left my purse..."

He cut me off. "It's on me. Drink." He held his goblet up. "Arbour Ale. Best around Ignius." He tipped the glass rim to his lips, pulling in a mouthful of ale.

Sitting there, he appeared to be ordinary—extraordinarily handsome, actually. I wondered what the mysterious man was up to. His lips curled into a teasing smile.

"Are you trying to lower my inhibitions?" I asked, breaking my silence.

Music filled the room and voices shouted above it. "Is it working?" He replied playfully, bringing the mug to his moist lips again.

I took a sip before answering, swishing the cold drink around in my mouth. The flavor was refreshing and cool, yet sweet. I eyed the goblet and took another swig. It was delicious.

"Not yet." I matched his playfulness. Two could play at his game and I wanted information. I didn't know how long I'd have before Ghost would bless us with his presence.

"Thanks for the drink. So...what was your name again?"

It was hard to hear over the crowd and music, the volume drowned out his deep voice, so I angled my head as if I couldn't quite hear him. I only hoped he hadn't realized he never told me his name.

His hand wrapped around the goblet and the overhead light highlighted white scars that snaked across his fingers and hand like veins of a river branching off a map. I choked on my drink. Tears pooled in my eyes. For a second, disbelief held me in place, as I remembered the exact scar on the man where I'd been detained. He was the man I immobilized, the one who offered mint tea and stew in the dark room. *Luke,* I thought it was. Luke was his name. Hidden by the shadows then, his face wasn't as I had imagined.

"Are you alright?" A genuine look of concern crossed his face.

I cleared my throat. "Fine. Thanks again for the drink." I lifted my glass, took one last long pull and placed the glass down a little too hard. Standing to push back the chair, he grabbed my wrist. I hurried to think of an excuse to leave.

"Won't you stay for another?" He was charming, I'd give him that, but there was a reason he wanted me to stay. I didn't know why, but I needed to get out of there. I knew who he was, and eventually he would figure out who I was, too, if he hadn't already. That deep gut intuition told me he knew exactly who I was though. "I have a date. Sorry," I replied, pretending to be oblivious.

Just as I stepped away, a fairly tall woman and a broad shouldered man, headed toward the table from the other side of the room. I strained to move away quickly, but my steps were altered and sluggish.

"Luke. Where have you been?"

It was the woman who spoke. Was she the one who had said I should have been left in the Rouche to die?

The room had grown crowded making it difficult to exit. Anxiety picked up and my legs began to shake, my arms hung at my sides like heavy lead. Between the pulsing fluorescent lights and the hypnotic musical beat, my head began to swim and my vision blurred. I felt like a ragdoll, pushed and shoved through the crowd like a child's toy. The room had an eerie vibe and gave me an unsettling quiver in my gut. Sweat beads formed along my forehead. I tripped, stumbling into a tall brute of a man. My hands lazily went up, as if moving in slow motion, landing hard against his fur vest. I peered up to a hideously contorted face. Oversized lips moved but nothing came out. He laughed exposing large rotted teeth the color of dung. I opened my mouth to scream but was cut off quickly. A viselike grip yanked on my arm, wrenching me away from the crowd and hauling me into the shadows.

THIRTEEN

Blood and fiery heat rushed through my veins, into my head as it lolled side to side, bouncing around with building warmth. "I think I gon puke," I slurred. My arms dangled like noodles and thumped against something solid.

"Quiet," a strained voice said.

"You no tell me quiet. I'm the foss. Boss, I say. Did you hear me, fungus?"

I poked a finger on the hard lump. "It'ss not so hard, it smooooshy."

"You sure know how to inflate an ego. Maybe I should have left you back there."

I pried a sluggish eye open, only to close it right away. "That's twice."

"Twice, what," he said with a grunt.

"Twice I wasss told I should be left. Nope. Thas no true.

Threeee times." My lids peeled open to slits. Moving my fingers to my eyes, I counted down. "One: Orphanage. Two: Luuuke. Three: You. Yep, thas tha-ree."

The jostling abruptly stopped and my head bounced against a stone-hard wall. His body stiffened.

"Ouch, fungass." My heavy eyelids opened. The smooshy hard mound was someone's rear-end. My eyes wouldn't focus clearly, but I knew a derrière when I saw one. Folded over a shoulder like a sack of potatoes, the blood rushed to my head and the nausea had become overwhelming.

"I'm gon-be-sick." My numb fingers touched my numb lips as if they would stop the sickening urge. "I can't feel. I gon be sick, dammit."

Just as my feet reached the ground, my body slumped to the floor, my shoulders hunched in and I retched. Tears escaped my eyes as the convulsions shook me. Circles were drawn along my backside and sections of hair tucked behind my ear. The spinning wouldn't stop and I thought my death was certain. "I gon die." My lips quivered.

Coldness seeped into my palms and knees. The noises dissipated, all except the shallow breaths as I worked through the third wave of nausea.

"He got you good," he whispered. "Just a little farther, okay?"

I stuck out my arm to stop him as one last wave of vomit spilled from my mouth. An arm wrapped around my waist and legs, and swept me up gently, cradling me snug against his chest. I was in the arms of a man I didn't know. Or did I?

A CLINK ROUSED me from my dreamless sleep. I ached all over and my mouth felt full of thick, dry cotton. My lips smacked, wishing for water. Hesitantly, I peeled my eyes open to thin narrow slits—heavy as my helmet bag. I was lying in a bed near a brick wall. My eyes moved over the room without recognizing anything.

A form pulled from the shadows of a screen. "It's you," I rasped, making out the female's face. "That's a pretty shade of purple you're wearing. However did you get it?" I flopped back down, resting my arm across my eyes. "Where's G?" I rasped. "I know he's here." I tried to form saliva and to my dismay, I was fresh out of liquids.

"Water's on the stand. And a pain pill. Get it yourself," Pria said, and smiled bitterly. "He'll be in shortly." She spun on her heel to the door.

"I don't like your tone. Get him now." She didn't hear me; her booted feet were already an echo away past the door. I wasn't surprised to see Pria in the least, but I hadn't expected her to be my welcoming committee. And I was glad to see my art work worn on her face. A smile lit my lips. I rolled to my side to get the cup and waited for my eyes to adjust, and my blood to circulate.

Dark hued beams ran the ceilings length. A simple nightstand, chair, and a changing screen were the only furnishings. A quilt supplied the only true color with splashes of inky blue, swirls of violet, and ivory accents. It was all very bland and boring. Not even a window to look out, a magazine to scroll through, or a phone.

I swung a leg over the side of the bed with a groan. I closed my eyes, still feeling dizzy. The residual effects from the ale had a hold on me. "How did this happen," I said to myself, pulling in a deep breath. My bare feet touched the cool wood below and I steadied myself. A woodsy pine scent permeated the room. I hadn't had but one ale and shouldn't have felt so ill. Sluggishly, I maneuvered to the doorway and glanced at the paneled door that lead to who-knew-where and slowly twisted the handle. Quietly, I stepped into an empty hallway lined with brick walls and intermittent iron sconces emanating a weak glow. Shallow voices drifted around the corner to the left. I peered around the edge, hesitated, the curiosity getting the better of me, and followed them.

Faint light pooled below the gap between the door and the wooden floorboards ten paces away. I tiptoed over to the sealed door, pressed my back up against the wall, and sealed my ear against the panel. Ghost and Pria spoke tensely in hushed tones. It was wrong on so many levels to eavesdrop, but my legs turned still while my head and heart collided in a battle of wills.

"She's your distraction. Distraction will cloud your judgment and that distraction will get you killed." Pria spoke with force but I could tell she was trying to keep her tone down.

"Stay out of it, Pria."

"I don't do well with people telling me what to do. You

know that, Grady."

"And I don't do well with people I care for getting hurt, or worse. I need to get her out of here. Luke already knows she's here. If he goes back, informs Ignius brigades she'll be hunted down. I won't risk her safety. She's my responsibility now."

"Why would you think Luke knows anything about her? Have you seen or talked to him since you've been back?" Her voice came out strained. "Luke would never turn you in. But, I am intrigued by how much she matters to you. Why bleed over a girl that can never be yours?"

Did I hear her call him Grady? Maybe it was another pet name of hers. And did he just confess to Pria he *cared* for me? My cheeks warmed at the thought. Could Ghost truly have feelings for me? I heard movement and shuffling of feet and my body stiffened, ready to bolt at any sign of their departure. The hall was empty and quiet, but my pulse thumped in my ears, intensifying the dull headache.

"Grady, people you told you'd protect needed your help. You weren't there. You were off in another country and I needed you here."

What was Pria talking about? I didn't trust her from the moment she stepped into the cabin. There was no love lost there. But her words were spoken with real emotion. Then something Ghost had said struck a chord. How did he know Luke, and what others? There were too many pieces to a bigger puzzle I couldn't seem to fit together. It was obvious Ghost and Pria had a history, but I had a hunch there was more to it. She loved him. It was evident in the way she looked and spoke to him and she saw me as her competition, a threat. I wondered briefly, if he ever confessed his feelings to her or if the love was unrequited.

A floorboard creaked, startling me. I scanned the room,and to my relief no one was there. I felt like a trespasser lingering behind the wall, listening in on their private conversation.

"Pria, I'm sorry. I'm sorry I wasn't here for you. But you know I had no choice. My position doesn't sanction a choice." His tone hardened. Right then, an uncomfortable feeling of dread washed over me, dread of him loving her back.

"We have to get him back, Grady. We have to do something," she pleaded. "People just don't go missing in Terrapin. I know those men in the cove have him, and I'll do whatever it takes to get him back. *Whatever* it takes."

Who was she talking about? People missing? *Who* was missing? The cove she mentioned—it's where Ghost and I witnessed the small army of men quarrying stone, and I had sworn I would never go back, even if it wasn't where I had been detained. The moment I spotted the scar on Luke's hand in the brew house, I feared I'd be taken away, back to the dreaded campsite, back into the hands of my captors. He said he wanted to help me, but there was nothing stopping him from delivering me the same fate as Rucky.

The murkiness in my head slowly cleared. Ghost said he was from Terrapin but I hadn't given him an opportunity to tell me his side of the story. My emotions got the better of me. And I knew better. Pilot training taught me to separate myself from my emotions and I failed. I should have controlled myself.

If this island was small enough, it certainly was possible Ghost *could* know Luke. I shifted my weight, and pressed my ear to the wall despite the uneasy feeling in my gut.

"I notified a few friends who I think can help you slip through Ignius and into Scoria without being noticed." Pria sighed. "But first, they want your word that if anything should go wrong in the plan, you won't hold them accountable, and your collaboration with us would be backed by Amani. As her heir, you will be representing Scoria on her behalf. Do I have your word, Grady of Scoria?"

For a few unsettling moments, there was silence. Then, Ghost spoke. "I can't make that promise, you know that. Leave Amani out of it, she has nothing to do with this. I'll take my chances, be held accountable for Jinx and I. But should anything happen to you or your men...that's on you, Pria. Take my word or the deal is off."

I couldn't hear what she murmured to him, but I was sure I felt her anguish through the wall.

"Then it's settled. This conversation is over. I'll meet with them, and then I'm getting her out of here." His frustration came through loud and clear.

I released the breath I had been holding. Whatever this verbal contract meant, it had to be important. Knots bound my stomach, I didn't want to get caught eavesdropping. The screech of a sliding chair raised the hair on the back of my neck. Turning quickly, I slinked back to the tiny room replaying the conversation over in my mind. I tried to push the thought out of my head for now and focus on getting back to Nordic, but it was impossible. The more I pondered the idea of playing third wheel to Ghost and Pria, taking up residence in this lion's den lacked appeal.

It was only minutes before a knock came at the door. I adjusted myself on the bed busying my hands in my hair. "Come in," I answered. Ghost's dark brown eyes peered over the doors edge. I wondered what he agreed to. And what Pria meant by *heir*.

I wound three strands into a loose braid and dropped it over my shoulder. "You took long enough. So, let's cut the crap and get down to it, please, because I'm sick of the mysteries and the lies." I shifted my body and stretched out my achy legs.

Sliding the chair beside the bed, Ghost settled into the seat. "Alright, we'll do it your way. I owe you that much. But first, answer this: Why would Luke want to drug you?"

"What makes you think this Luke guy did anything? And how would you know his name?" I shot back. My head tilted, glaring at Ghost through slanted eyes.

His fingers combed through his hair. He cleared his throat, shifting his weight in the chair. "Don't play me for a fool, Jinx. I was there last night. Who do you think carried you out of the brew house?" He leaned forward, his voice softening. "I don't understand you. It wasn't enough for you to be shot down, detained, and know your being tracked, but for you to run off was irresponsible. I assumed you were sensible. Now, though..."

"Go on," I urged.

"You should be afraid of what's out there!" He pushed up from the chair, his face flushed with anger, a vein standing out on his temple. If I provoked him enough, perhaps his lips would loosen, spilling the complete truth.

"Why?"

"After I told you your name was on a hit list I thought it would be blatantly clear. Someone wants you out of their way. They could have killed you!" He glowered at me a moment longer before falling back into his chair, exhausted from the exchange. "There are two territories in Terrapin: Ignius and Scoria. Currently, we are in Ignius territory. I, however, am from Scoria. Pria and Luke are from Ignius, and Luke is good friends with Pria's stepbrother, Maru." He shot a glance over his shoulder to see if I was following. Ghost's leg pulled up, his ankle rested over his knee. He clasped his hands on his lap and for a moment, I thought he was finished speaking.

His eyes were incredibly dark and rich. It was easy to get lost in them. "Let me get this straight...Luke, Pria and Pria's stepbrother Maru, are friends, and they are from the territory we are currently in."

He closed his mouth and nodded. "Maru and I met at a very young age, before his mother and Pria's father got together. I accompanied my parents on many visits, on my father's insistence. Anyway, we became good friends growing up; we went through a lot together. The cabin in the jungle...we built it together." His voice trailed off with the memory. "It was so long ago. After..." his brows pinched, and rolled his shoulders and neck.

"After what?"

"Nothing." He cut me off quickly. "We would meet when we

could, work on it for hours on end. It was an escape, a place for us to get away and be boys. Not long after the cabin was mostly finished, Maru brought along Pria and Luke to show it off. Pria is less than a year younger than Maru, and since they were stepsiblings, they got along like friends more than anything."

"So answer me this…if you know Luke so well, what would be his motivation to drug someone he doesn't know? I hadn't told Ghost that wasn't my first encounter with Luke, or that I swore Pria had been behind the bar before my ale had been served. Whatever their relationship was, I felt it was best to stay away from the subject until he brought it up.

"He would never…" he said, more to himself than to me, "be that careless." Luke had an opportunity to do with me as he pleased while I was locked up, and he hadn't touched me, even said he wanted to help me. He admitted he knew I was from Nordic, and if Ghost and Luke were childhood friends as he said…that was reason enough as to why he demanded knowing if I was alone. He feared his friend was shot down, too.

"There was a time when Pria and I were close. I knew she had developed feelings for me, and at one time, I had for her, but I knew eventually I would have to leave and those feelings would dissolve over time. Mine did, hers didn't."

My arms pressed down on the mattress and hoisted myself up straighter, wrapping my arms around my knees. We sat in companionable silence for a minute, until I looked at him and said, "The initials at the cabin…those were yours." I knew they were deep down, as well as the knife I found. They were Pria and Ghost's symbol, etched into the wood like two young lovers.

He nodded his head without hesitation. I bit my lip, considering. He left Terrapin under duty and obligation, but came back for me. Tentatively I said, "Are you truly over her?" I knew I was walking on precarious ground, but this was the most honest conversation between Ghost and me since being on the island.

He stared at me intently. "When word reached base of an unfortunate accident and you never showed up after training, I *knew*. All I could think about was you, your face, every morning, night, and in-between. I never felt that way with her." He ran a hand down his face, releasing a breath. He looked worried, afraid he had confessed too much too soon. He did care for me and if he were the man he seemed to be here—considerate and caring—not the guy I knew in Nordic who was there on false pretenses, maybe I could care for him, too.

"I need to know how you were able to join Nordic Airre without getting caught. Nordic has state-of-the-art technology."

He shifted in his chair, resting his elbows on his knees, and clasped his hands together. He seemed to be weighing his words with carefulness, perhaps with caution. "We have plants in Nordic. It's the only way we can keep Terrapin off their radar... which is precisely why I was there, to deflect any possible threats, not steal information or plot against them."

Interrupting I said, "You're a freaking spy?" The words flowed smoothly like motor oil. This all seemed ambiguous. There was too much to process. He told me everything, down to the very last detail. Somehow, Ghost and many others had managed to slip past the eyes of the Nordic Advisors and

Commander DeMarco for decades, selected into the Forces, and other venues, remaining hidden and undetected by the best in Nordic. *Unbelievable.*

I slipped off the bed and paced. My mind was like a kaleidoscope of thoughts—twirling around and around. I spun on my heel and marched over to him, braced my hands on the armrests and stared into the depth of his brown eyes. "Who are you?" There was enough venom in my tone, I almost flinched myself. Heat radiated down my body and my arms shook with anger. Our eyes locked with determination and something else.

Ever so slowly, Grady removed my hands from the chair arms, stepped away from me and paced from one side of the room to the other, the struggle darkening his flawless, tanned face. He wanted to tell me, but was afraid. I stood perfectly straight, and focused hard on controlling my temper so I didn't shake.

He nervously stopped in front of me, then he lowered his dark brown eyes to gaze at me. "I am Grady Allen Duchane, heir to the Scorian Territory."

FOURTEEN

I turned away stunned, gripping a bed post, my jaw clenched tight, wishing I was in my jet, away from here, away from Ghost or Grady, or whatever the hell his name was, and his stupid island. I tried not to overthink the logic too much, but he might as well have slapped me across the face because that was what his words felt like. It would have been easier on both of us if we had put more effort into trusting one another with our pasts to begin with. I gave him a sidelong look.

"You can keep calling me Ghost if you want," he said quietly. "It's kind of grown on me."

My hands trembled. I could tell myself it didn't matter, that none of this mattered, but it did. I knew him as Ghost the pilot for years, not Grady. Grady was some freaking heir of a country I hadn't known existed, and I was stranded on it with no way out which was precisely why I had to do something. Being here, close to him, complicated everything, clouded *my* judgement. I closed my eyes, pulled in, and slowly released a deep breath in an attempt to stay calm.

"Jinx?" His voice wavered. "You can shut down. But, please don't push me away." He paled but looked into my eyes. In that instant, it was hard to remember he hadn't always been this guarded, secretive guy. Maybe it stung a little, but I knew why he didn't tell me before now. He was protecting me from knowing too much and protecting this island from people who would destroy it. But I wasn't there to destroy it, I just wanted to get off the island. Back to the life I knew and away from the painful memories that landed me here.

"When you sent the comm, and I know it was you, you told me to 'trust no one.'" I looked away for a moment. "I guess that meant you, too," I rasped, struggling to find the right words. My brows pulled in. "Luke," I said, swallowing hard, "your *friend*, was one of my captors." I released my death grip and stepped back, crossing my arms.

"No." He fiddled with a leather band circling his wrist. A small greenish stone mounted between four silver prongs. "Are you positive?"

"At first I wasn't. But when I saw the scar on his hand, and heard his voice it all became very clear. Once I pieced it together, that was when I got up to leave the brew house. And, well, you know the rest."

He cracked his knuckles; a vein pulsed in his neck. "There is no one you can trust more than me. Never forget that."

How was I supposed to believe him? Deep down, I wanted

to. My instincts told me he meant what he said, but he had already kept vital information from me. Regardless if it was a protected secret, if he wanted me to trust him, then he should have trusted me, too. Mutual respect goes both ways.

"I'll get to the bottom of this." His tone deepened, "And when I do, you won't ever have to fear him again." His dark eyes went cold and hard. I had never feared Ghost, but in that moment, I would hate to be Luke, or anyone crossing his path. He stood up and stormed to the door.

"Gho…, I mean, Grady?"

He paused at the door, not looking at me but down at the knob.

"He didn't hurt me. If anything, I hurt him."

"Across the hall is a bathroom. A change of clothes is behind the screen. Get cleaned up and dressed. I'll be back shortly." He fled through the door and slammed it shut. I flinched. I had never seen Grady so angry. How had the roles reversed so quickly? I pressed my palms to my eyes and let out a huge breath. My shoulders ached, and were tight with tension.

Warm water rained down on me. I closed my eyes, tipped back my head, and let the warmth flow over my body and rinse the thoughts from my mind if only for a short time. The air smelled of something soft and floral. I lathered the soap and rubbed the flowery pink suds over my skin. I stood underneath the stream longer than needed, but it was the first shower I had had since before I left Nordic Airre. I rinsed out the soap, and squeezed excess water from my hair, then coiled a towel around my body.

The tiles beneath my feet were cool to the touch as I stepped out from the shower. Prickles danced along my skin. I wiped fog from the mirror and examined myself. The dyed purple streak Casper put in my hair had washed away, and a thinner version of myself stared back at me. My collarbones were prominent as were the dark circles under my eyes. I finished drying off, pulled on the cargo pants and tank top, tucking the useless comm inside a pocket, and braided back my damp hair.

I crossed back into the tiny room with the clothes I stole and set the folded pile onto the floor beside the changing screen. A plum colored backpack caught my eye, settled against the leg of the brown chair. Curiously, I looked over the bag and unzipped it. Inside the pack was my tattered flight suit, but the knife with the engraved initials was missing. I pulled the top of the suit from the back and trailed my fingers over my embroidered name still clinging to the material. It seemed a lifetime ago since my jet went down into the murky Rouche waters.

Without a doubt, Luke knew who I was and where I was from, but he had not mentioned how. The memory was vague and diluted by time and injury. My coiling thoughts lacked clarity, but I could have sworn he wasn't alone, nor were they agreeable on what to do with me. My brows pinched. I tucked the flight suit back into the pack when the door swiftly flew open. I flinched at the sudden noise.

"I see you found the bag I left for you," Grady said, slowly closing the door behind him. A bowl of bread and cheese filled his other hand and he set it down on the bed.

"Yes, thank you." I paused, sat the backpack down and

looked up to meet his eyes. "I have a question for you…"

"Ask away."

"If you *truly* are an heir—and I'm assuming privileges and power come with it—why are we going through this trouble? Why didn't you take me to Scoria right away and secure a way back to Nordic for me? Why drag this out any longer?" I couldn't help but notice the confused look on his face as if he couldn't understand why I would ask such a question.

"Sorry, you caught me off guard." His smile wavered.

He swept out a hand, motioning for me to take a seat. I moved the bag aside and pulled myself up on the bed. "I feel like a prisoner," I whispered under my breath to myself.

Grady pulled up next to me, his leg grazed mine. A fluttering sensation tickled my stomach at the contact. Heat warmed my cheeks and I looked down busying myself with my nails. I could have cared less about them, but I couldn't look him in the eye. My body's response to Grady betrayed me time, and time again. I should have been angry, but his presence carried a calming effect.

He had no idea I overheard his conversation with Pria earlier, but nothing made sense to me and I needed to understand why there was a meeting in the future with friends of hers and why we were supposedly sneaking out of Ignius and why we would be *hunted*.

He released a deep breath. "I brought that food for you, you should eat," he said, motioning to the bowl beside me. "When I got word your jet went down, I immediately checked the tracking device link. The monitor system I created confirmed you survived. Of course, once the water broke through, tracing was impossible. The location was lost near the southeastern waterline, which is Ignius' territory, but close to the Scorian/Ignius territory line." He paused. "Are you following me?" he asked, sneaking a quick glance.

I nodded. "Yes."

He rubbed his hands down his thighs and placed them behind him, leaning back. "The airstrip is shared between both territories. Both Ignius and Scoria have men operating it. When you saw me at the airstrip talking to those men, I learned Ignius members were already aware of your presence. By that time, I had already procured arrangements to get you out. I knew there was a chance I wouldn't find you in time or the Ignius Brigades would already be out searching for you, but I had to try anyway, regardless."

"The boat," I said, with understanding.

"Yes," he confirmed. "I had planned on getting you safely away from Terrapin without either parties knowing, but when you fled from Luke, someone within his circle broke their silence and convinced Ignius officiates of a rogue who posed a threat to them..."

"But I'm..."

"Wait. Let me finish." He held up a hand, not looking at me. "When they were notified—I'd assumed what they were told wasn't the truth—they were convinced that this *rogue* had something to do with missing Scorians and Ignians."

My head whipped to the side and my jaw dropped.

"If I am caught with you in Ignius Territory, especially

now they are aware of you, I'd be detained and investigated... possibly go to trial. And since I am the heir to the Scorian Territory, implications would elevate between the Ignius and Scorian treaty."

Not only had Grady put his neck on the line for me, he put all of Scoria there as well. No one had ever done something so brave and selfless on my behalf. I was an orphan...a nobody from Nordic. And he risked *everything* for *me*. My heart sank. If I could erase the conflict and pain that etched his eyes, I would have. I reached back, wrapped my hand around his and gave it a comforting squeeze. There were no words to express what his sacrifice meant to me. For the first time in my existence, I understood what unconditional truly meant. And I wasn't so sure I deserved it.

"Thank you, Grady. I can only imagine the position I've put you in." I looked down at the wooden floor. My chest ached.

"Don't blame yourself, it's not your fault, Jinx. You were just thrown into the crossfire. Don't ever apologize for something you had no control over. Besides, it was my choice to come after you and I knew the consequences and risks involved. It was completely my choice, my free will and I don't regret it."

We sat silently for a moment. The words Grady spoke when he found me 'I came for you' crossed my mind. As angry as I was with him for holding back the truth, I couldn't hold that against him. If anything, he was only trying to keep me safe, and I finally realized there was more to him than his sexy smile and beautiful brown eyes. I had feelings for him.

"So what do we do now?"

"Pria has arranged a meeting with friends who are willing to help us get out of Ignius. I want this meeting to run smoothly and without you two at each other's throats. Stay away from Pria, Jinx. She'll extend a hand in friendship and stab you in the back with the other." He pushed away from the bed and reached a hand out in offering. I took it. It was warm but gentle.

I consumed a few pieces of cheese and bread quickly on his insistence before we left the room and worked our way down a narrow hallway. Our footsteps stayed in rhythm as we wound a corner and up a narrow stairway to a heavy wooden door and into another blank hallway.

"Where are we?" I glanced at Grady.

"We're in an extension behind the shops along the main road in the village. It's a quick way to get from one end to the other unseen."

I thought about that for a minute. What a very clever engineered plan. I also could see it used as a way to slip people in and out unnoticed. If Pria arranged this meeting, that meant she had access to the hallway as well.

"Can you access all of the businesses on this side through this passage, or just a few?"

The dark carpet soaked up any noise from walking, but the buckles on Grady's boots clanked lightly with every step. The only light came from the overhead fixtures but they dimmed in comparison to the suns natural light.

"No, not all of the businesses do, only two. Pria's great-grandfather had this built when they constructed this building. He was an engineer and developer. Actually, she comes from a long line of contractors."

The carpet wasn't worn; actually it appeared fairly unused, except for a faint stain barely visible at the top of the stairway where stone flooring butted up to it. There were not any other exits from the outside, only a few steel doors on the inner wall.

"So, where did we just come from if it wasn't a business?"

Grady glanced at me. An odd expression crossed his face. "We were in Pria's private living quarters. The bedroom you were in is below ground level, but there is an upper level. From the street side it appears to be part of a shop, a wall separates them."

Our strides stayed steady. Grady's hand brushed mine as his arms moved between our bodies. He smelled of fresh clean linen with a dash of something woodsy. His hair had grown out, which made me wonder how long I had actually been on Terrapin.

His steps slowed, I matched his pace then he came to a stop. He turned and looked down into my eyes, his hands reached out, pulling mine into his. Butterflies tickled my stomach at the gentleness of his warming touch.

"We're here. Remember, when we go in there just keep quiet and let me do the talking. Okay?" The pads of his thumbs worked soothing circles on top of my hands.

"Fine," I confirmed with a sigh and rocked back on my heels. "Let's do this."

FIFTEEN

I followed behind Grady like a second shadow. I wasn't sure what to expect when we walked through the door. A line of circular fluorescent lights bordered the ceiling, each one surrounded by glowing blue stones. I had never seen anything like it before, and I wondered if maybe Pria's great-grandfather designed that, too. Again, the room was windowless but lit well enough they weren't a necessity. I ached to feel the sun's warmth and the smell of fresh air.

Grady pulled a charcoal gray leather chair out from behind a blackened wood table that horseshoed and mostly filled the center of the room. The air was stale but smelled of rich leather. He motioned for me to sit. I preferred to stand, but I sat halfheartedly and gripped the armrests for support.

There was no one in the room besides Grady and me. He pulled out the chair next to mine and settled into the leather confines. I rubbed my palms down my thighs and glanced over at Grady. His wandering eyes roamed around the room, as if searching for phantom cracks in the walls. He didn't appear uneasy, but he was good at hiding his emotions and I knew him well enough by now that he was anything but comfortable.

The door opened swiftly and Pria stepped in flanked by two men in all black pants and shirts. Pria glanced our way then took a seat at the head of the horseshoe. The men were of average height and build. The first man had light facial hair lining his jawline and a constellation of freckles peppered his face, his strawberry-blond hair was short with spikey tips. He took the seat adjacent from Grady, comfortable, like he'd been here before. The second man had a stockier build, and appeared pale in contrast to the waves of raven black hair. His rounded face mirrored that of a child's and when he smiled at something blond guy said, his eyes were swallowed into the cheeky folds.

An elbow nudged me to attention. "Huh?" I asked, looking back to Grady.

"Pria just said we are still waiting on one more."

I glanced at Pria and back to Grady. "Okay," I whispered back.

I didn't know why I spoke quietly. I felt out of place and honestly, Pria made me uncomfortable. I could hear her sharp, painted nails thrumming along the table as if impatient and bored. She was having a conversation with blond guy. Clearly she forgot to tuck in her girls as they bulged from the top of her shirt and on display for everyone to see. Her voice was full of bluster and her laugh was arrogant.

"Would anyone like a drink while we wait on our last to arrive?" Pria asked.

I flashed a dramatic smile, tossed my braid over my shoulder. "I don't know if anyone else would, but I would love one. Grady?" I shot him a seductive smile. I just hoped it didn't look as awkward as it felt.

"Sure, sounds good," he said, grinning like a fool. A pang hit my heart. I couldn't help but let my barrier release and melt into the leather chair.

Against the wall, a panel slid away revealing a mini wet bar. Long stemmed glasses hung from the inlet's top. Along the back wall behind a tiny sink were shelves lined with goblets and crystal tumblers. Below the sink were shelved bottles of various shapes and sizes, full of colorful liquids. Pria went to work mixing drinks and plopping cubes of ice into crystal tumblers.

Grady was in a conversation with baby face and blond guy. I hadn't realized my leg bounced until Grady's hand slipped under the table and placed it on my thigh, squeezing it gently. He left his hand rest on my leg while he continued talking with the men. Warmth seeped into my leg below his hand, spreading through my body with a thrust of its own as if it craved his touch. I wondered how his lips would feel against mine, if they would be gentle and soft, or hungry with demand. I remembered the tender kiss he placed on my forehead. It was tender, sweet. Could he really be more than the playboy I knew him to be in Nordic? My heart was restless and told me yes. I wanted to believe it badly.

Pria moved around the table distributing drinks from

a silver tray fluidly and with practiced efficiency, not a drop sloshed over the rims. She placed Grady's mug down, then practically poured herself onto his lap, her chest inches from his face as she leaned across setting a mug down.

"You'll love this Arbour Ale, Jinx. It's the best Ignius brew around," she crooned.

I stared down at the repulsive amber liquid. A bitter taste filled my mouth. My mind replayed my first encounter with Arbour Ale in agonizing detail. I offered a watery smile wishing for anything other than the Ale in front of me. There had been plenty of other options and Pria had served me the one drink I couldn't stomach.

"Let's make a toast, shall we?" Pria raised her glass. Grady and the two men followed. I hesitated then forced myself to participate. The frost coated mug did nothing for my sweaty palms. Grady must have noticed my hesitation. A flicker of concern crossed his face. He began to speak when Pria cut in. Her red painted lips shimmered in the light matching her nails.

"To new friends and old, I have known many, liked not a few," she tittered, "loved only one," eying Grady, "I drink to you."

What the hell kind of toast was *that*? The others took deep pulls from their glasses. I raised mine to my lips holding my breath and took a swig. The cold liquid flowed into my mouth. I swallowed, but almost choked. I wasn't sure, but the Ale had tasted different somehow. I coughed and set the mug down. Water filled my eyes and heat flooded my head.

"Are you alright, Jinx?"

I was slightly bent over by that point and Grady had placed an arm across my shoulders and leaned around my supporting arms with a concerned look on his face.

I pulled in a deep breath and blew it out. "Yeah, went down the wrong pipe is all," I murmured. That had been my excuse last time, too. Had I just made a complete fool out of myself? I was not going to give Pria the satisfaction of my weakness. I pulled myself upright, wrapped my fingers around the mug and downed the entire damned drink. And it felt liberating.

The others were slack-jawed. Then, fist bumps and felicitations rang through the air by Pria's cronies. I surprised myself, but I held back my smile.

"Well then," said Pria as she wiped away invisible particles from her shirt, obviously not amused by the encouragement. Even beneath the tanned skin, redness surfaced on Pria's face.

She swayed her hips back to the bar to fill drinks. If she thought shoving her chest in Grady's face and shaking her rump would improve her chances, she was sorely mistaken. I knew what I overheard and Grady admittedly confessed he had feelings for me. However, I was no better than she was by shoving innuendoes down her throat, even if it did feel good.

Grady handed over a full mug. I wished he had chosen a different drink, but I hadn't had a reaction this time so I reached for it. "Thanks."

"Take this one a little slower. I don't need to carry you over my shoulder again, alright." My knees went weak at his half-mooned smile. He knew it wasn't the amount I drank that night, but a drug ingested. And despite the tension in the room and with Pria's blazing glares, I could still smile back and know all would be okay.

We sat around the table making small talk. Grady's hand rested on my knee again. His gestures were smooth and confident, and I didn't berate myself or him for it. It just felt right.

I began to wonder if the other man she mentioned was going to show up. My patience was wearing thin. Grady and I could devise our own plan to slip out and run back to his cabin or even to Scoria. We didn't need Pria or her entourage.

"Sure thing."

I knew nothing about Pria's lackeys or their involvement with her. They spoke maturely but joked around like typical young men. I had never guessed ages well, but wondered how old they were.

"Nice of you to finally join us, Linkin," Pria said, obviously annoyed.

Grady's body went stiff, and then wrapped a firm hold around my wrist before I could turn toward the door. His face went pale and ashen; a sickly expression replaced his smile. Dread filled his eyes as he looked over my shoulder. I twisted in my chair to see what caused his reaction. My body tensed, my vision tunneled and I sprang from the chair, flipping it onto its back, and barreled toward the man with a guttural roar.

My face was inches from the murderous fiend who failed to kill me. A cluster of arms pinned mine down to my sides. My body was lifted to be hauled back, my leg shot out with a winding kick to Rucky's face. My muscles strained against their hold, battling to get free.

"Get him out of here!" Grady demanded, struggling to pin me down.

"I'll kill you, you son of a bitch!" I said, as spittle flew from my mouth. "You traitor! Let me go," I screamed, tugging and pulling at arms and kicking my legs. Angry tears rushed down my cheeks. "I hate you, I hate you. Let go of me," I shouted repeatedly, trying to pry the fingers wrapped around my body. The iron grip cinched, and I couldn't breathe. "I hate you," I said between sobs, my voice raspy and weak. "I hate you."

My head dropped between my shoulders, sinking into the swaddled hold, and gently pulled to the floor.

"Get out of here! All of you," Grady demanded. "Shh. Calm down, I'm here," he whispered, brushing back damp wisps from my face. His breath was cool against the warm tears. It was Grady's voice. He held me firmly against his body, enveloped in his strong arms.

"He tried to kill me," I said, my words hitched. "Kill him, Grady," I pleaded. "Please. Do it for me," I begged. My head curled into his shoulder. Numbness encompassed every fiber, every nerve ending. I couldn't fight or say the words I practiced many times over if I had the chance to come face to face with Rucky again.

My eyes closed as if they could shut out the horrible pain clawing its way out from within; shielding me from everything that ever tried to hurt me—to break me—the images of the mean boy at the orphanage, the ugly words spoken to me as a child, and the man who tried to take my life. I was wrecked and broken. The wall of security had finally crumbled. I was hollow.

SIXTEEN

Grady rocked our bodies, whispering soothing words into my ear only I could hear. I was all out of tears and stared numbly at the circles he brushed over, and over again on the top of my hand. I followed the path with heavy eyes. For me, the pain wasn't over, and I hoped over time my scarred heart would mend.

The room was still and quiet. I didn't want to open my eyes and face the world, face the man who did this to me. My heart ached. It wasn't much of a life I was living and nothing made sense anymore. All I wanted was Grady to keep holding me and I was going to hold on with whatever I had left. He shifted, his motion breaking my reverie.

"Stay," I rasped, holding on a little tighter.

"I'm not going anywhere, Jinx. I'll stay as long as you need me."

His words warmed my heart. I felt a light flutter on the side of my head, a butterfly kiss. I closed my eyes, soaking in the feeling that came over me—the first touch of life brought back into me since…I didn't even want to say the name. I didn't want to step back into the deep dark ominous hole I was slowly creeping up from.

Grady pulled his outstretched legs up. I craned my neck back to look up at him. He looked down with red-rimmed eyes. "You don't have to say anything, Jinx." A lone tear broke free, wiped away by Grady's finger. Our eyes locked as if they were speaking the millions of words we wanted to say, and in that moment, Grady's hand swept through my hair and his hand cupped the back of my neck, pulling me in to him. Our lips and bodies melted together as if a force of unspoken languages were speaking to us, calling us to one another. Our lips met softly, and then increased with urgency. The euphoric feeling and pleasure cloaked me. I rotated into him. My hands roamed through his hair and over the curves of his chest, back, and arms. A moan escaped his throat, feeding my desire. Large warm hands brushed the bare skin between my top and the edge of my pants, pushing the tank top up and over my head. Kisses trailed below my ear and cascaded along my collarbone, between my breasts. His hands splayed across and up my back, kneading as they explored every curvature and angle. He gently guided our bodies onto the carpeted floor, our lips sealed. Heat trailed down my body and burned at his fiery touch.

"I'll never let anyone hurt you again," he rasped between kisses. His confession pulled me back to reality with brutal force.

"Grady. Stop. We have to stop," I said, breathlessly. I pushed up on my arms and rolled off the top of him, sweeping up my tank top. His breaths were heavy, matching my own.

"I don't know what bothers me more—your iron will, or that you're gorgeous and half naked."

I laughed because it was either that or weep. I slipped the tank top on, pulled my hair from its braid and shook it out, and wound it into a bun. I drew my knees up, resting my elbows over the top trying to calm my breathing. *What are you doing you idiot! He will use you, and then dispose of you like dirty laundry, like your mom.*

"Did I do something wrong," he asked, voice wavering.

I shook my head. "No." *Yes.* I turned to him. *Cut him off now!* I needed to look into his tawny eyes. "You did everything right. And that's why I you need to leave." His head flinched back slightly, giving me a blank look. My chest tightened. I reached for his hand. Our fingers laced together.

"I can't leave if you push me away first, am I right?"

Suddenly, our laced fingers were the most interesting thing I'd ever seen. *You coward!* I cleared my throat. "I'm just going to come out and say what's on my mind." Squaring my shoulders, I met his eyes. "You're right, Grady. It is easier to push you away. You do things to me..." I took a deep committing breath and released it. "You stir up feelings inside of me I've never felt before and honestly, I'm not sure what to do with them. It scares the hell out of me. No one has ever, uh, no one has ever made me think the things I..." I look down at our entwined fingers again. I'd never had a loss for words, but sitting there in front of Grady I couldn't gather coherent thoughts. "I don't want whatever this…" I motioned my hand from me to him and back. "Whatever this is going on between us to…"

"To disappear?"

I nodded.

Grady tilted my chin up, his fingers brushed down my neck as he released a heavy breath, relief washed over his face. "I told you, Jinx. I'm not going anywhere. I meant that. I will be here for as long as you need me…" He paused, "As long as you *want* me. So, whatever *this* is…well, I know what it is," he said, pulling up our twined fingers, kissing the tip of each knuckle. "And in time, you will, too." His hand cupped my cheek. My eyes closed and I nestled into it.

A knock at the door broke up our moment. I smiled a true smile at Grady. He stood up, reached a hand down to me. I wrapped my hand into his and he pulled me up from the floor, and gave me one last kiss. A fleck of light danced in his beautiful brown eyes.

The impatient knock came again, a little harder this time and I realized we were alone. Everyone scattered like roaches after the attack. And I wondered if they would bring Rucky back in. Seeing him again nearly ripped my heart out. I saw the flames shoot from his jet, rupturing into a blazing inferno. No way could he have survived the massive flames that engulfed the jet. Suddenly, I remembered Pria called him Linkin.

"Have a seat," Pria said, waltzing in. Her voice dripped with calm firmness.

A lump formed in my throat, and the walls seemed to close in around me. I just wanted to be safe. I wanted my friends safe, and I didn't want to run anymore. I gathered my courage and walked back to the table. We all took a seat. The soft leather chair was a relief from the hard, carpeted floor. I rubbed the bridge between my eyes.

"Jinx, I can't have you maiming my guys. Falsely accusing Linkin of trying to kill you is not only going to screw up the plan, but it will trigger unwanted enemies. And as of right now, it appears you have enough. Linkin is a good guy. Obviously you have him confused with someone else."

Her nails tapped against the table, raising the hair on the back of my neck. "Let's just get this over with." I was too worn down. "If he's not Rucky, and I still say he is, then let me ask him questions."

Grady stared at me with concern. "Are you sure you're up to this right now?"

"Yes. Definitely."

Why hadn't Grady reacted as I had? Why wasn't he furious or disgusted? It didn't make sense. Maybe that thought was drowned out by my attack? I wanted to find out. A few minutes passed, the three men hesitantly strolled into the room and took a seat. My body charged with nervous energy. My knee bounced beneath the table. I hesitated. The longer I avoided the conversation, the more I would risk him not understanding why I did what I did, and Pria was right, as hard as it was for me to admit it. I certainly didn't need any more enemies. He was obviously upset by my actions.

"You remind me of the man who tried to kill me," I said. "He looked so much like you, and I thought you were him." My heart hammered as I waited for him to say something back, like I was mad and delusional.

He looked away and back.

"I had a twin brother, Ledger. But he died when we were young."

Grady placed his hand on my lower back. The resemblance was uncanny. And there was no denying Rucky was his twin.

"No, he didn't."

"Yes, he did. I saw it with my own eyes. My father took him into the Rouche. And he never returned. No one ever does."

"No?" I repeated softly. "But he did, and I did, too." I knew he wasn't going to believe me. Why would he? But I was walking proof, couldn't he see that? He didn't know me, but he had to know Grady, or at least of him. I turned to Grady. "Tell him."

Pria broke in. "This is preposterous. You must have hit your head damn hard on the water. There is no way that this *Rucky* person is who you say he is. No way. Impossible."

I immediately stood, anger surged through me, pointing my finger at Pria. "Don't *ever* interrupt me again. And I know, Grady knows, I'm speaking the truth." My arms and legs shook with fury.

"Let me introduce myself." Grady cut in, standing tall with his chest out and chin held high. "My name is Grady Duchane of Scoria, and what Jinx said is the truth. And if Rucky was your twin, Ledger—and there is no doubt in my mind he was—then your brother, in fact, was alive."

When he spoke like that, I wanted to grab him and do things I wouldn't speak of, but thought about more than a few times. I felt a sense of pride. Grady was in a stare down with everyone at the table. He meant business. His deep authoritative voice sent tingles down my arms and legs. "If you question her,"—he looked down at me and back to them—"then you question me."

If Linkin was Rucky's or Ledger's twin, then why was he in Nordic? How was he cleared and chosen as a pilot for Nordic Airre? Why not go back home to Terrapin?

Linkin, who was the very image of Ledger, began to pace the floor. Pria busied herself handing out mugs of Ale, while downing her own, replacing it with another. My brows furrowed. I didn't notice until then, her agitated disposition. She seemed distracted. Maybe hearing of Linkin's dead twin affected her.

"My objective is to get Jinx into Scoria. Rumors have spread, and I'm asking for confirmation…" His eyes raked over the room. "Have there been random disappearances—in *both* Scoria and Ignius?"

"Deklan. Tell him," Pria said, her tone strained.

He took a few deep swigs from his mug, his dark blue eyes roamed past everyone. "It's no secret, Grady, Amani's health has receded. Without your physical presence in Scoria, your people have been an easy target."

"Wait." Grady held up a hand in warning. "How many?"

"We don't know for sure. It's been through word of mouth. With the seasonal change upon us, fewer are traveling to the trading post. The trees are shifting up on the mountainside, people are settling in for the Change."

What was he talking about? Trees shifting? Trading post? And who was Amani exactly? I overheard Pria mention the name between her and Grady earlier that morning.

I looked up at Grady. "What is he talking about?"

"Jinx, Terrapin has seasonal changes. What you've seen up to this point will eventually morph into frigid condition with a lot of snow. Our vegetation shifts and molds itself to sustain the climate changes—a chameleon of sorts. What Deklan was trying to say is that, the mountainside plants have already transformed, and the change is swiftly sweeping into the valleys. There's a trading post between Scoria and Ignius, much like the markets in Nordic, or the Trifecta, except ours aren't open during the White Change."

I rubbed the tension between my eyes. "Let me get this straight," I said, gathering my thoughts. "Your trees and everything green will just...the weather manipulates their appearance? They mold into something else?" My voice raised an octave.

Terrapin had many more secrets than I had ever thought possible, but this had been unexpected. I couldn't wrap my mind around the idea that the climate changed, the vegetation altered in appearance. It all seemed too bizarre.

"Yes, exactly. And now that the change is happening, our time is limited to find out where they have gone, who took them, and why. But before I can do anything, I need to go to Amani."

Pria cleared her throat. "We can leave tonight, after sunset. Deklan, Linkin, Max and I will come with you. And besides, I would love to see her, too. It's been too long. She was always so kind when we went to visit her together."

The temperature in my body shot through the roof. There was no way I was agreeing to her terms, or her traveling with us. She had already made her intentions very clear, and it was a recipe for disaster.

Grady didn't have a chance to respond. Linkin cut in, his eyes trained on mine. "Do you know where my brother is? You said he shot your jet down. Why would he do that?" He ran a hand down his face. "It doesn't make sense," he muttered under his breath. "None of this makes any sense."

As much as I hated Rucky, er, Ledger, I couldn't dismiss the throb in my chest. His expression said enough. He lost his brother once and honestly, I didn't know if he survived or not. I didn't have an answer to give him.

"I don't know." I looked down at the empty glass in front of me. I didn't know what else to say, and I couldn't meet his eyes again. They were a replica of his twins and I hated him with all my heart and soul.

SEVENTEEN

Two black all-terrain style trucks pulled up near the back entrance, facing the dipping sun. The windows were black as tar. Deklan stepped from the first truck and opened the back door as if ushering us in. Out of habit, I looked up to Grady. He gave me a quick wink and pressed a hand to my lower back steering me forward. I looked both ways as I hiked up my backpack strap and shuffled to the truck. I hunched against the cool breeze tickling my bare skin. A few flickering street lamps casted a dim light and shadows danced off the brick walls of the alley.

Pria trailed behind Grady, splitting off toward the second truck. I glanced over to the other truck. Linkin stood with a hand clasped around the driver's side door. Max walked around the backside of the second truck wiping his hands off on a tattered rag, tossing it inside the opened door.

I glanced back at Grady. It was as if he read my thoughts. "Silencer." He cracked that sexy lopsided smile at me. My heart skipped a beat. "We're trying for the discreet exit strategy."

I slid my bum across the seat, making room for Grady and his pack and let out a deep breath. I shrugged off my backpack and set it on the floor by my feet for easy access. Once again, I was going into new territory blinded. This time I had my wingman by my side, I wasn't alone.

Deklan shut his door behind him as he adjusted the rearview mirror and slipped something into his pocket. He put the keys into the ignition and cranked the black beauty to life. By the look of the meaty truck, I expected a deep rumble, but it was silent as a kitten. We rolled forward down the alley and turned off into the dancing shadows. I wouldn't have believed the story about Terrapin's peculiar weather but as we crept passed the streetlamps down the main strip, I discerned subtle changes to the plant life—minimal, but some nonetheless.

Leaves skittered passed the windshield, yellow, orange and red blurs of color sailed by. They moved and shifted, like my thoughts. Grady placed a hand on my thigh, warmth spread beneath his touch.

"You look tired. Here." He adjusted in the seat, setting his pack on the floorboard and pulled me into the crook of his body, wrapping his arm around my shoulders. "Much better," he whispered brushing back wisps of hair. A light sweep of his lips touched the top of my head. A flitter in my stomach replaced the pent up nerves.

I rested my head between his shoulder and his chest, feeling the rhythmic beats of his heart. I had never felt someone's heartbeat. It seemed like a silly thought, but it meant something to me. Grady had crept his way into my own heart and I was afraid I realized. That, at any time he could walk away and I would be another heartbroken challenge obtained. I pushed the doubts away from my mind and focused on Grady's woodsy scent permeating the space around me. The vibration and sway of the truck lulled me to sleep.

My body was tossed up from the seat jarring me awake. My arms flew out searching for something to grab ahold of. Grady must have fallen asleep too. His body went stiff. His arm shot out grabbing onto the back of the passenger seat, the other across my waist.

"What the hell was that, Deklan!" Grady hissed. "Why aren't we on the main track?" His neck craned behind us and back to Deklan. "Answer me!"

Deklan swiftly pulled the truck into a hollow off the two-track. "Shit!" He slammed a hand against the steering wheel. "We hit a large pothole. I think the axle is bent. I'll go check it out. Stay here, I'll be right back."

The black of night swallowed the moon's light. Headlights from the second truck grew brighter as they pulled up behind us. The lights glared through the tinted glass. Globes of gold specks invaded my vision. "I can't sit here. Let's check it out. Maybe we can help."

Grady followed me to the back of the truck where Pria, Linkin and Max stood. Deklan rounded the back of the second truck hauling a flashlight in one hand and a tool kit in the other. The temperature had dramatically dropped since we had left Ignius. The nights I had slept in the jungle alone were warm and humid.

Pria intentionally stepped around the guys and found a spot next to Grady.

"Seriously," I muttered to myself.

"Are you alright?" Pria questioned. "Deklan tried to veer around the hole, but it was too late."

"We're fine, Pria." My tone didn't mask my irritation. She was directing her concern toward Grady. It was obvious Pria hadn't given up on him and I guess I would do the same had I been her, but I wasn't and she continuously wormed her way in to steal his attention. She was stubborn, something I could relate to but hated to admit it even to myself.

Grady stood with his arms crossed, facing Pria. "Why aren't we taking the main route? This isn't what we talked about. This route will add a couple hours to the drive and I don't have that luxury right now."

Anger penetrated the space around us. His heated stare was unavoidable. Pria placed a hand on his shoulder and spoke in a calming tone, "I should have told you before we left. I didn't think it would be a problem. A landslide blocked the road. It's impassable. I changed the route at the last minute, Grady. Please don't be angry with me."

I couldn't take anymore of Pria's batting eyelashes or cooing. I slipped away, knelt down by Deklan's legs. Grunts and clanking of tools against metal emanated from beneath the truck.

"How's it looking?" I questioned, taking a peek.

"Not good," he said exasperated. He pulled out from beneath the truck wiping streaks of dirt from his backside and hands. "The axle is bent. It would be pointless to drive it on this track, it's too rough."

Coming up with a practical solution to our problem only elevated my anxiety. Pria, Max and Linkin agreed to take the damaged truck back toward Ignius. Pria would then swap transportation and meet us at Amani's. I still was uncertain who Amani was to Grady but I had an idea. We were exposed. *I* was exposed and it didn't settle well. If the men truly were searching for me, would Grady, Deklan and I be able to ward them off alone? And it didn't make sense that Pria would leave so easily when all she's wanted to do was pull Grady back into her grasp.

We went our separate ways. Grady's disposition unsettled me. He sucked the edge of his lip as he gazed out the window. I placed my hand over the bump in my cargo pocket steeling a little comfort from the communication device I couldn't part with.

There wasn't a radio to break the silence or music to keep my mind off all the terrible images of the past. As if Deklan read my thoughts, hard slow beats filled the cab and I was thankful for the disturbance.

The rough two-track jerked the truck side-to-side, our bodies rocked violently with the motion of the truck.

"I'm pulling over. My stomach isn't agreeing with me." Deklan veered the truck just onto the edge, put it in park and jumped out. "Hang tight. Shits," he said between pinched words, as if straining for control, and rushed off holding his stomach.

Cringing, I said, "He didn't look too well. Should one of us take the wheel?" I felt bad for the guy.

"Might not be a bad idea. I'll drive. I know where to go."

The music had the same sultry beat I heard in Ignius. It was hypnotizing yet soothing. Grady's body relaxed into the seat. His hand circled mine and lightly tugged me toward him. I followed his lead, scooting up beside him. I could feel the heat seeping into my body.

"Who is Amani, Grady?" I looked up to meet his eyes. There were too many things I didn't know about Grady and Terrapin and what the future held for us.

He took my hand and inspected it. A chill went through me as he traced a finger over the tiny scratches left on my hand. One corner of his mouth went up into a half smile, and my heart seemed to think it was one of the most beautiful things. I reminded myself of who he was and how we got to where we were.

He cleared his throat. "Amani is my great-aunt, and has ruled Scoria for as long as I can remember. She will like you," he said with a smile. "She's the wisest woman I have ever known. You remind me a lot of her."

I felt a flutter in my chest. Women never liked me, but I suppose that was partly my fault. I didn't give them a chance; I hadn't given anyone a chance until I met Casper. I thought of the orphanage and the loneliness I felt there. I was a number, a rejected misfit with no one to call my own. I could see the warmth of Grady's love for Amani in his expression. When he talked about her, there was a shimmer in his eyes, a fondness and respect.

I turned my head, shielding my face behind my hair. I was ashamed of myself for realizing too late I wasn't as strong as I thought I was. I was a coward who hid behind a front, because if I shut people out and kept them away, I would never be hurt or lonely again. I was wrong. I had always been lonely because of my ignorance.

Grady told me he would be by my side as long as I wanted him, needed him. And maybe my heart knew before my mind, but from the moment he found me, I wasn't alone and I did need him. If only I could insert a wall between my brain and my mouth. Grady peeled through my rough exterior and planted an emotion I could finally admit to. Ardor. There was so much power in that tiny little word.

"What do you think?"

"What?" I had been lost in thought.

"Deklan. He should be back by now."

"What should we do?" I muttered, gazing out the window. "Go look for him?" My gut clenched at the thought. "You don't think he got lost in the dark do you?"

"I doubt it, but I'll walk around and see if I can find him. Stay close or inside the truck until I get back, okay?" Grady said quietly. "I can't imagine he went too far. He looked to be in pretty rough shape."

The temperature dropped inside the truck without the extra body heat. I wrapped my arms around myself and waited while Grady circled the perimeter. It was a guy thing. My foot bounced on the end of the center counsel as the minutes ticked by. Where was he? Just as I went to pull the door handle, Grady beat me to it.

"Has Deklan came back?"

"No, he hasn't. Should we call out for him?" After the words left my mouth, a lump formed in my throat. I didn't want to attract any attention. And I couldn't imagine others would be milling around in the vast crazy jungle at that hour. Then I remembered the men combing the beach. It had been late into the night or early morning. A cold chill poured through the open door.

"He should have been back by now."

Grady's concern ignited a spark of worry in the pit of my stomach. I slid across the seat and looked into the depth of his dark brown eyes highlighted by the moon. "Let's find him and get out of here."

EIGHTEEN

I took one last glance at the stars twinkling so bright in the sky and wished I could have joined them to escape the dark thoughts assaulting my mind—of all the horrible possibilities—of what potentially could have happened to Deklan. He'd been gone too long. I placed my fingers into Grady's outstretched hand. He wrapped it firmly around mine as he helped me out of the back seat. I had no idea where we were going, and I didn't know what to expect, what we would find. But I hoped it was Deklan with his pants zipped up, treading back to the truck, unscathed. I shook my head, banishing the image. This place did things to my psyche.

The jungle floor sloped down, uneven. I held onto a small tree to sturdy myself. The fringed bark transmuted into something flat and shield like. Not how I remembered it. The vegetation *had* morphed into something different, something stronger. I wanted to ask Grady all the questions pent up inside, but I knew it wasn't the time or the place. The last time I demanded an answer, I threw a hunk of wood against his back, and the reception was not pleasant. I thought better of it and chuckled to myself.

"This was the direction he went, wasn't it?" he whispered, unsure if we were going the right way. "We entered the same spot he did. I'm positive."

Night creatures' eyes glowed, an eerie silence broken by a labored groan. The pounding in my chest quickened as Grady and I tore off in the direction of the noise. My shoulder smacked into a tree.

Grady was faster than me. He sprang ahead as if he wore night vision goggles and could see through the thick dark.

"Jinx!"

I heard Grady's warning shout. I pumped my arms faster, jumping over a downed tree branch until I came upon dancing shadows. I came to a sudden stop and my breath hitched. Grady was in the middle of a heated brawl, throwing down another figure. He was strong, stronger than I expected. "Get Deklan," he said, blocking a punch.

I narrowed my eyes, swiftly searching for Deklan. He groaned again. Grunts and fists went flying. Grady could defend himself, but I had to get Deklan to safety. I skirted around the two men fighting, slinking low. Deklan's body curled into a fetal position, his hands covering his face.

"Shh, Deklan. It's me, Jinx," I said hovering over him. I tried to move his hands to get a good grip, but he fought against me, crying out. A metallic tang filled the air. Blood. I pulled back my hands, my eyes widened. The crimson slid between my fingers and coated my palms like a glove. They were slick with Deklan's blood. My heart slammed against my chest, the air expelled from my lungs.

"I'm going to wrap my arm around you. I'll take it nice and slow, but I need your help," I said quickly. "It's going to hurt, but I have to move you. On the count of three, I need you to push. Okay?" I was worried about Deklan's condition. I couldn't tell where the blood came from or how severe his injury was. Without a doubt he had internal injuries by the amount of blood that dripped from my hand, it was deep. I wiped them off on my pants and positioned myself.

"On the count of three. Here we go. One…"

I squatted down, tucking my arms under his armpits.

"Two."

I let out a deep breath.

"Three."

A heavy shoulder slammed into my side. My body pitched forward, smashing hard into a tree. My breath forced from my lungs. Tears streamed down my face. I bit back the pain and blinked the stars from my eyes. The palest thread of predawn light lighted the figure as it leaped toward me and it was too late.

Fingers curled around my arms, and swung me around. I braced myself for the next blow. I struggled against their hold, taking a shot to the gut, then another. I deflected the next punch with my arm and swung a leg up, connecting my knee to their ribs. He cried out, and I turned to run but an arm snaked out, and wrapped me in a stronghold. A cold, sharp blade pressed against my neck. I shifted my feet, and the blade slid deeper into my skin. One misstep and it would score my flesh. Thick arms tightened, drawing my back flush to his heaving chest, dark scruff scratched my ear.

"Where do you think you're going little girl? I figured you perished in the wreck or drowned. I was eager to see you dead."

My body froze. I knew that voice...that dark, malevolent voice.

My eyes narrowed. "And I was eager to live and get revenge, Rucky. Or should I say, Ledger?"

He spun me around. Pink scars and damaged blistered skin covered his face. His nose and lips were disfigured, but there was no denying whom that voice belonged to.

"You were supposed to die, bitch." Spittle flung from his mouth, his bloodshot eyes bulged with hate. "You think you're clever. You're nothing but an orphan, a loser." He pressed the blade's tip below my jaw with more pressure.

His words stung. *How did he know I was an orphan?* It didn't make sense. He pulled his face beside mine, rubbing his ruined skin against my flesh. "Feel that?" he asked, pressing harder, his breath reeked of decay. "That's nothing compared to what I am going to do to you." His maniacal laugh rang in my ear. "I remember you, Jinx. I remember your braids and the purple ribbons tied to their ends..." He ran a hand down my hair, curling a strand around his finger, "And when you turned me in. But, you see..." he trailed off, clenching my hair in a tight fist. "Your juvenile tattling backfired." He licked the side of my face. I shuttered, and closed my eyes. My heart pounded in my chest. It couldn't be. *No. It was impossible*, I thought as I pulled in a breath. *How could it be?*

"You're finally figuring it out aren't you? I'm surprised you never pieced it together, but again, it happened so long ago."

"I understand now why your lunatic father left you to die in the Rouche. You were a terrible son, an embarrassment to your family, and you haven't changed. You're just like him, aren't you?" I rasped, trying to get under his marred skin. His vicelike grip loosened at first, shaking his head as if he could hardly believe I knew *his* secret. He quickly recovered and in that moment, I was scared for my life.

"I enjoyed watching you squirm every day at the academy— looking over your shoulder, wondering if the guy next to you might touch you..." I felt him run a steady hand down my sternum, sliding down to my waistband. I sucked in a breath, twisting to distract him but his grip tightened and knife dug deeper as he continued, "Pushing people away with your tough exterior."

Keep talking, you bastard. Keep talking until Grady comes.

"I was adopted, and you spent your childhood inside a caged-in yard like a filthy animal. I bet you're wondering what I might do to you right now. Will I take you, you ask. You see, I've thought about this for a very, very long time. Submit to me and I'll make it quick, just like I did..."

"You bastard!"

"Shhh. Let's not make this more difficult than it has to be, accept your fate. Face it, *Charlotte*, you've lost."

Silence.

"You," I said, as I realized why he had always been vindictive toward me. It was personal for him.

"That's right, *me*."

"You're just an older version of the little pervert who attacked a young girl behind a shed. My telling on you didn't backfire, Rucky. If anything, it worked. You left and I never thought of you again. You'll never be seen as anything other than a criminal and a traitor." Beads of sweat trickled down the center of my back. "Why did you do it? Why did you shoot my jet down? Was it to get back at me for getting away, turning you in? Your pride stripped away from a young, innocent girl?"

He scoffed. "Is that what you think? You honestly believe I care about that?" He laughed.

"Did you ever wonder why boys were adopted before girls? We were *chosen*...selected for something greater than anything you can imagine."

I tried to pull back, but his hold was too firm. *What did he mean?* I searched through my dark past, the years spent as a number, not a human being. And it all came flooding back. What he said was true. I remembered watching those whom I believed were the lucky ones walk through the metal double doors and into a life I had always wished for. Boys of every age throughout the years waving back at the hopeful faces plastered against the glass windows, longing for their turn.

"Why? Why are you doing this to me?"

"Because, people want you gone," he said, gritting his teeth.

"You know too much…" he trailed off. "But don't worry, Jinx. I came here to finish the job."

I did not have the fighting skills of the ground troops, but I knew well enough my time was up. I mustered all the fear, hate and rage inside and drove my knee as hard as I could between his legs and sent him slumping to the ground. I kicked up again, and again. The knife flew from his grip and slid down the hill. My arm cocked back, connecting with his face. He screamed out.

"This is exactly what winning looks like," I spat, punching him again. "And don't you dare speak my name you piece of shit."

Deklan's painful cry pierced my ears.

I kicked Rucky in the face one last time and took off toward Deklan. My feet were swiped out from under me, and my body crashed against the forest floor. Something hard dug into my lower thigh. I yelped, scrambling to get away. My nails ripped through the packed dirt, as my body was drug down the incline, grasping for anything to latch onto. My legs thrashed against his hold.

"Help!" I prayed my plea would be heard.

Finally, a leg came loose and I twisted my body enough, landing a blow to his neck. Rucky fell back, but quickly recovered. My feet slid against the loose debris as I darted away. Tears choked me. My body jerked back. I lost my balance and fell to the ground. My forearm deflected a hard object, sending a wave of pain down my arm. I recognized the cool object, wrapping my fingers around the wooden handle, hiding it beneath me. My body flung around. Rucky straddled me, pinning me beneath his weight.

My mind raced with the possibility of rape and of death.

"You can't get away. You're dead," he said between gritted teeth. His arm cocked back. It was now or never. I thrust the knife into his sternum, pushing up with all my might. A sucking sound reached my ears. A metallic tang tainted the air around us. His eyes grew wide and he wrapped his hands around my shaking ones, fighting against me. Rucky's grip loosened, his arms dropped to his sides, his body wavered and crashed to the ground like a fallen tree, motionless. Still.

I stared at the body, frozen in place. *What had I done?*

A fresh blanket of blood coated my trembling hands and fingers, dripping heavily onto my pants. My breath hitched, my blood went cold. I had never killed anyone before, not even as a pilot. Simulators were different. They didn't count, not like this. All the training in Nordic Airre could not have primed me for the emotions an actual death caused by your very own hands created. I looked over again at Rucky's lifeless body, the knife embedded inside him, my lungs fought for air.

A twig snapped nearby. I jumped to my feet, pulled the knife from the corpse, and steeled myself for battle. A silhouette moved across my sight. I whipped around toward the shadowed figure. Grady appeared, looking relieved. And I blinked the sting of tears from my eyes, the knife slipped through my bloody fingers to the ground with a thud.

"Are you alright?"

Words hovered on the tip of my tongue. Numbness spread

through my body, easing the sharp pain in my chest. I just pointed to the lifeless form at my feet. His eyes flicked to Rucky's corpse, and for a moment, I thought he would rush over, wrap me in his arms, and tell me I would be okay. That killing someone in self-defense was different from coldblooded murder.

"Jinx, we have to get rid of this body," Grady continued, oblivious to my torment. "And get Deklan help. Grab the arm and leg and I'll take the other side." He positioned himself, his fingers clasped around an ankle and wrist.

I closed my eyes. "I can't do that." My voice came out shakier than I wanted it to.

"Jinx." His voice laced with frustration. He shook his head and walked to me. "Where's the Jinx I know? The tough girl who kicks ass and takes names, huh?" I teetered between confession and silence. He slightly shoved his hands against my shoulders, pushing me back two steps. "Let it out, get pissed!"

"I am pissed! But…I killed a man."

"That's where you're wrong. You hear me? Look in my eyes. You killed a traitor. Got that! A traitor."

NINETEEN

The pain in my hand and ribs were replaced with worry as I stared down on Deklan's bloodied and battered face. *That could have been me.* A wave of dizziness made my head spin. I strained against his dead weight as he leaned into me, tucking his arm over my shoulders. I breathed in deeply. It smelled of coppery blood. Everything seemed tainted with crimson.

The wind picked up and Deklan moaned in protest as I adjusted my grip. The weight steadily eased up as Grady slid an arm beneath Deklan's shoulder. He let out a breath. "We need to hurry. I don't know if they will be back or if there are others."

"Did you...did you cover him well?" I wasn't familiar with the laws of Terrapin, but in Nordic, murder was the worst kind of crime. *It was self-defense,* I told myself over and over. Rucky's last words were 'you can't get away. You're dead.' He meant what he said. His tone was undeniable. He was going to murder me. If I hadn't killed him first, it would have been me buried beneath the changing vegetation and a wild animal's next meal.

"The only living things that will find his body are the animals." We moved as quickly as we could without agitating Deklan's pain further. The groans emanated from a deep place, and my heart panged with every wail and cry.

We made it to the truck and carefully placed Deklan across the backseat, his face lit by the overhead light. Mounds of raised flesh disfigured his features into a giant glob of purple and red hues, extending beneath his shirt, which was torn and smeared with blood. His moaning stopped but I couldn't help but worry for the battered guy. He could have internal injuries and we had no way to medically treat him until we reached Amani's in Scoria.

Surprise lit my face as Grady opened the truck door for me. "Thanks."

The road was rough, jostling our bodies around, making the headlights dance around like a spotlight on a stage. Grady's death grip on the steering wheel eased and he slowly slid his hand over mine, weaving our fingers together. He looked over. "Are you okay?" he asked.

My body was still shaking from the adrenaline, but I said, "I'm fine."

It was a lie, and we both knew it, but I couldn't think about Rucky or what I had done. It would consume me.

"You're shaking," he said, but what he really meant was, "You're lying." And I was. I lied through my teeth to protect myself from opening up the proverbial floodgates, my self-defense mechanism—shutting down, turning away with a steely cold heart. As much as I didn't want to bring up Rucky or even think about him, or the awful things he'd done, his words grated on me and I needed release. He didn't press the issue, but kept his eyes on the road with a weary, sorrowful expression.

"Grady, this may sound crazy, but Rucky said something before I..." I couldn't finish the sentence. I took a deep breath and exhaled, wiping sweat soaked palms across the crusty dried blood on my pants. "He said something that, at first, didn't make sense, then I realized what he said was true."

Grady snuck a glance at me. "What did he say?"

I took a deep breath. "He said, 'Did you ever wonder why the boys were adopted before the girls? We were chosen...selected for something greater than anything you could imagine.'"

Grady's arms stiffened. He remained silent and his silence unsettled me. "What do you know that makes them want to kill you?" he mumbled more to himself.

"What?" I eyed Grady, unsure I understood what he said.

"Nothing. Just thinking out loud."

I waved it off, but filed it away in my head. "It's true what Rucky said. Repeatedly the boys thinned out from the lot. It was very rare girls were adopted. "

"Do you remember what Rucky was wearing?" Suddenly the thought hit me. If he was working with the rogues, perhaps there would have been a symbol or a badge of some sort linking them together. The men who came to the cabin had a blue stripe circling their bicep. The darkness of the forest turned everything to black. If he had worn a stripe, it wouldn't have been noticeable.

Grady denied seeing a stripe, but the idea of "what if" turned my stomach inside out. I winced as the truck jerked, hitting a large pothole, holding my sore ribs. I peered over my shoulder at Deklan's still, lifeless form. One thing was certain, though: we knew more than we should have, I was meant to die in the plane crash, I knew who attempted to kill me, and I knew orphaned boys were strategically adopted steadily to be unnoticed. A chill rushed down my body. I survived. And I'm their worst nightmare. My jaw clenched, anger bubbled to the surface. If it was my silence they wanted…then they'd have to kill me first, and I wouldn't let that happen. If it had to do with Grady and I, maybe we could figure it out together.

Did Grady being with me put him in danger, too? I squeezed his hand, taking in the comfort of him beside me. I tilted my head back and felt the heat of the rising sun through my closed eyelids—drinking in the warmth through my skin. It was a new day.

TWENTY

Someone shook me awake. I rubbed the sleep from my eyes. I craned my aching neck toward Grady, forgetting I'd been punched and smacked into a tree. A hiss escaped my lips. I raised a hand before he could say anything. "I'm fine, just a little sore." He looked disheveled. His hair was askew, dark circles penetrated the skin below his eyes, and his bottom lip was swollen—cracked with dried blood down the center.

"Are you okay? I'm so sorry I fell asleep." I hadn't noticed his split lip in the night. Then my mind went to Deklan. I twisted around carefully and found a pale, bloodied body. My eyes watered and I covered my mouth with a shaking hand. He looked horrible, barely recognizable.

"He's still breathing." Grady's voice was gruff. "He's been unconscious. He isn't feeling any pain right now."

I turned back toward the windshield. "Where are we?"

I studied in wonder at a home carved into the side of a mountain. A powdery white fluff gathered around edges and corners, fusing to the leafless branches of the trees. Ice hung in a sparkling fringe from the branches and tapered in uneven ridges to a spear-sharp point. A thin white sheet blanketed the emerald green landscape.

"Safe. For now."

What did he mean by that? "Aren't we in Scoria? Is this Amani's?" I looked to him through nervous eyes. His were vacant and so very far away. I placed my hand on his and leaned toward him. "Grady? Are we at Amani's?"

His jaw worked back and forth. "No. We can't get to her if she's down there. I hope her informants got her out in time." He looked down at his hands. "Whoever *they* are…they have managed to create a roadblock, blocking the only road into town from this side of the mountain. Armed men surround the barricade. Lucky for us it was sunrise and the lights were off on the truck." He turned his sad eyes to me. I could see the frustration behind them, the uncertainty written on his face.

"I'm so sorry, Grady. Did we get away unseen?" My heart sank and I couldn't help but think it was my fault. All of it had been my fault. I had never met Amani, but I knew of her importance to Scoria—to Grady. She was his someone. And now she was in danger's grasp and there was nothing I could do to make it better, to fix the chaos that had become my life, and pulling others in with it.

I caught his gaze with mine. "It isn't over Grady. We'll devise a plan. We will get to her, and then stop whoever is behind this.

They will be held accountable. Is there anyone we can trust to help us?"

He pinched the bridge between his eyes and let out a deep breath. "No, they didn't see us, but that doesn't mean they don't have others combing the forest. Let's get Deklan inside and then we will discuss this further."

I hoped he would confide in me. I wanted to be someone he could depend on, someone who he could trust unconditionally. I twisted to open the truck door and Grady stopped me.

"Wait."

I paused.

"He didn't hurt you, did he?" His eyes raked over my body for any signs of injury. There was only one, buried beneath the surface. My heart clenched at the thought of Rucky, what he said, and the blood drained by my hand. And the anguish Grady was so obviously going through—I wished I could steal his worries away, absorb them so he wouldn't have to feel that ever again.

"No. He didn't hurt me. I'm fine," I said, patting his hand.

The house was something of another world. A wall of windows of various angles lined the front, framed within solid rock, and tucked beneath an umbrella of snow coated trees and evergreens skirting the rocky-topped edge. Off to the right, a cave-like entrance opened up as he pulled the truck inside. Yellowish-white stone walls were lined with white tubes that directed natural sunlight deeper into the dwelling. The truck rolled to a stop beside an olive green all-terrain vehicle, even though we could have kept going through the tunnel. Metal linked chains rapped around the tires. I thought of the dirt bike and the chains I had seen before.

"This place is amazing, Grady. I've never seen anything like it. Where does this lead to?" I asked, curiously, pointing straight ahead.

"There's an opening on the other side of the mountain. There's a network of hidden tunnels in the mountain. This one leads to another exit if needed, but it's concealed, hidden so no one gets in but me."

I was instantly intrigued and wanted to find out more about this mysterious man cave.

"Let's get him inside."

Deklan's body temperature had dropped and he rested limply in Grady's arms. He was unconscious, which was for the best. His face had turned dramatic shades of purple and blue. His features were unrecognizable and bloated.

The door pulled open as we came upon it. I recognized the blue eyes staring back at me.

"Karrie," I said, as if asking a question. The strawberry blond smiled at my recognition.

"Come in quickly," she said, ushering us inside.

We entered through a stone hallway and down a series of steps carved from stone. Along the walls were the same fluorescent stones I'd seen in Ignius. I looked up in awe at the lighting and iron details as we made our way through another hall with earthy colored tiles lining the floor. We veered to the left and entered a bedroom. Grady placed Deklan carefully onto his back and withdrew the boots from his feet. Until he came to, we wouldn't be able to question him or obtain any new information. And being from Ignius, we hoped he knew or recognized his attacker. The room was spacious with natural hardwood floors.

"This is incredible," I said, sweeping my eyes around, absorbing the unique structure. It had a rustic feel to it. All stone, wood and iron. I looked above me in awe. Brilliant blue colored stones pelted the rock ceiling casting a faint light as if they were mimicking stars in the sky.

"What are those?" I asked in wonder. "I've seen them before. They're so beautiful."

"Next to you, they pale in comparison."

I gazed at Grady, my lips parted. Warmth spread over my cheeks.

I placed my palm over the stone wall, feeling the cool edges run over my skin. Specks of crystal dazzled under the lights.

"Welcome to my home, Jinx." Grady said, saddling up next to me by the doorway.

"Quite a space you have here. So this is where you grew up."

"It is."

Karrie vanished and came back with a bowl of water and a simple wooden box packed with creams, gauze, ointments, and oils. "Nice to see you again, Jinx. I'm Karrie as I assume you already know." She rung out excess water from the rag and gently wiped dried blood from Deklan's face. "He's been beat up pretty bad. It will take some time for the bruising to heal and the swelling to go down before I can tell if there is any real damage beneath the surface." Her short strands slipped passed her shoulders, fanning her face as she studied Deklan with probing fingers.

She pulled a syringe from the stash; her nails clinked against the glass tube. Copper freckles peppered her fingers. A steady stream of fluid sprang from the needles tip. "He won't feel a thing. These antibiotics should help with any infection."

I whispered to Grady, "How is she here?"

I looked up meeting his eyes. The dimly lit room turned them to a shade of runny ink. "She came with me, but we split up when I went looking for you." He smiled. I could sense the war raging inside of him. His sense of duty and obligation to Amani was where his heart was. We needed to devise a plan.

"Come on, I have something else to show you." He wrapped his fingers around mine and pulled me from the room. "Do you think Deklan will remember the attack? Maybe he knew his attacker."

"It's hard to say."

There were three we knew for sure, and the men at the quarry. Were there other roadblocks? And why Terrapin? There was no doubt in my mind either we had been followed, or set up by someone we knew. The coincidence was too ironic. Could it have been Luke? We traveled down a long lit walkway and passed a series of doors and open spaces, then entered into a very spacious living room. The outside wall decorated with windows had a view of the Rouche as far as the eye could see. Off to the right there was a loft built over a large kitchen and dining area, and across from that, there were a trilogy of couches, end tables and a matching coffee table. My eyes widened as I took in the spitfire redhead staring back through topaz blue eyes. "Casper," I whispered, blinking to clear my eyes.

"Jinxy!" she shouted, tossing a throw blanket aside, and sprang from the couch and into my arms. My jaw dropped. A tear sprang from my eye. My only friend, my roommate was in Terrapin.

"How are you here?" I mumbled over her shoulder. I pulled back, holding her at arm's length. "I didn't think I'd ever see you again. I can't believe you're really here. I missed you."

She pulled me close again. "I missed you, too, Jinx. I thought you were dead—we all did. I didn't think I would ever see you again either." She sniffled. "I'm so sorry what happened to you. When Grady told me what went down and he thought you were still alive…" Casper cleared her throat. "I wanted to believe him more than anything. It took some convincing, and when he told me about the 'hit-list,' it was all I had to hear. My decision was made. I went with his crazy plan to search for you. And here you are, in one piece, living and breathing, my strong-willed friend." Her voice cracked. "I'm going to kick whoever's asses did this. And then hand it to them."

It had been so long since I'd seen my friend, and looking at her now made me realize just how much I'd missed her.

Grady spoke up, "Why don't you ladies take a seat? I'll get us drinks. We have a lot to discuss."

I looked up to Grady. For a moment, I had forgotten he was there, and sprang into his arms. "I don't know how you did it, but thank you," I whispered. My chest tightened from the emotions taking over me. He was nothing like the man I thought he was.

I misjudged him from the moment our eyes met at the academy. I guess we were more alike than I imagined. We both harbored secrets and hid behind their illusion of security. I wanted to know more about him and Terrapin.

"You don't have to thank me, Jinx." He pulled back and locked eyes with me, and I warmed in many places. I licked my lips and he lowered his mouth toward mine. His touch was soft and teasing. I curled my hands into his hair, pulling him into me.

"You have a lot of explaining to do," I whispered.

It was time to get down to business, figure out why the rogue men were on Terrapin and what their motivation was. And why pilots were targets.

A throat cleared behind me. "We certainly do have a lot to catch up on."

My ears perked, and turned toward the accented voice. My eyes widened. A profound gut wrenching feeling swept through me. I studied her with the same amount of intensity and distrust as Rucky.

"Who's that?" Casper whispered over my shoulder.

I felt like I swallowed my tongue. Before I could grumble out her name, Grady spoke. "Casper. This is Pria, an old friend."

I looked over my shoulder at Grady, confused. How was it possible she made it to Ignius, swapped trucks and made it back to Grady's so quickly? And how did she know we were here instead of Amani's? I eyed Pria again, and noticed her more conservative attire. She looked strangely hurt, or annoyed. I couldn't tell. She gave a vague wave of her hand and set a bag down by her feet. "I apologize for interrupting. I left as soon as I changed out trucks. Where's Deklan?" she asked, her tone noticeably softer with a hint of sweetness behind it, yet traced with concern.

"Excuse me for a minute, ladies. I'll be right back." His hand swept across the dip in my back and ushered Pria down the corridor.

"Who's Pria?" Casper inquired, smacking me on the arm. I waited until the room cleared before I filled Casper in on all that happened, leaving out only the part about Rucky admitting he was the boy in my nightmares. Pria was a need-to-know basis, but she was back and Casper would need informed— warned, rather.

I sighed and pulled in a breath. "Casper," I said, exhaling, "She's a close childhood friend of Grady's. Get my drift?"

Her sky blue eyes widened. "She seemed harmless enough, though."

"Don't let her fool you. I don't trust her. She's been throwing herself at him since I've met her." Her reformed appearance and tone threw me off. Maybe she accepted Grady as a friend and nothing more, but I doubted it. He certainly did not lead her on and was clear about his feelings for me.

Grady strolled back into the room alone. He went to the kitchen, poured drinks and sat beside me, an unreadable expression on his face.

Casper stood up. "I need to use the little girls' room." Grady pointed her in the direction. The room was quiet. He turned to me and whispered, "Company will be arriving at any time. They will ask questions. Tell no one of your encounter with Ledger. Keep answers simple, but…" he trailed off, swiping a hand through his grown-out hair. "I know there hasn't been much time for us to talk and for me to answer your questions, and I'm sorry. A lot will be thrown your way…" He paused.

I placed my hand on his arm. "It's alright, Grady. I can handle it." I meant it.

The warmth of his breath sent tingles down to my toes. I nodded, not quite understanding why he wanted to keep that between us. Shouldn't someone know what happened? But if he asked for my silence, I owed him that much. "Alright. Who's coming?" I hoped we would have had more time to talk privately. I had so many more questions to ask him, and I wasn't sure how much Casper knew, or if I could confide in her. The need to get it out, to tell her everything I had been through drove me crazy. My promise to Grady won over.

His elbows rested on his knees, his hands raked through his hair. "Close friends of mine. They're like family to me." His hand wrapped around mine and squeezed.

Leaning over, I reached out, brushing back his fallen hair, and he turned to face me. We held a penetrating stare-down until he leaned in, brushing his lips across mine. My eyes closed, our kiss grew deeper. My stomach fluttered at his touch, my body warmed with every sweep of his tongue.

I pulled back, resting my forehead against his chest,

steadying my breathing. He cupped my chin, tipping my face up to his. "If you only knew what you do to me." A smile drew his dimple in. His silky brown eyes bored into mine while his other hand traced the curve of my waist.

My body went from 98.5 to an inferno in a matter of a second. *If he only knew what he did to me.* "Then why don't you tell me tonight after your company leaves. I think I'd like to hear what you have to say." I was shocked I said that. Did it sound as desperate to his ears as it had to mine? My cheeks warmed. I had never talked like that to a guy, but he cared for me, and it was clear I cared for him, too.

He pulled me in for another kiss. "Sometimes my actions speak for themselves," he whispered, his voice cut with emotion. The way he looked at me, with hope and desire, made my insides tremble.

"Well, that was an interesting toilet," Casper said, braking up the moment. She plopped down on the other side of me, as if she hadn't noticed the empty chair beside the couch. "Oh, I ran into your friend Prina leaving the bathroom. She said to tell you that Karrie was taking a break and that she would stay with Dexter."

Grady and I looked at each other and a burst of laughter erupted, a deep belly laugh, the kind that hurt our stomachs and cheeks. It felt so good, and almost foreign. And for a few wonderful minutes, we didn't think about the dangers that lied ahead. Tears rolled down our cheeks.

"What's so funny?"

Grady tried to right Casper between gaining his composure.

There was a sweetness to him as he corrected 'Pria,' not Prina, and 'Deklan,' not, 'Dexter.'

Casper laughed at herself. "It could have been so much worse."

TWENTY-ONE

I sat back and glued my eyes to the glass, anxious to meet Grady's friends, as headlights flashed across the windows, disappearing behind the rock wall. The sound of gravel crunching under tires as the vehicle rolled into the cavern-like garage hit my ears. I swallowed thickly. I looked from Grady to Casper, who had pulled up her legs, and chewed her nails like a meal.

"Stop that," I hissed, swiping her fingers from her mouth.

Grady eased himself from the couch and straightened his shirt. "Be right back." He smiled sweetly at me before he left. I followed him with my eyes until he disappeared.

A throat cleared. "You've got it bad," Casper whispered, shaking her head laughing.

She was right; I had it bad for Grady.

Footsteps echoed in the distance and my nerves began

getting the better of me. Minutes seemed like hours before Grady waved us over. He ushered us down the hall. I hadn't been this far into his home, and the farther we walked, the more claustrophobic I felt. We walked Casper to her room, promising to return after our meeting. A long burgundy rug ran the length of the hall, down a series of steps and finally to a large spacious room bordered by two large doors. We'd reached the bottom of the steps, a few feet from the open doors, and he pulled me to a stop. I turned to him concerned. "What is it?"

"Jinx," he whispered as he stepped closer, his lips near my ear. I tried not to breath him in too deeply because he smelled so good. "Once we step through these doors, there's no turning back," he said solemnly, giving me a worried look. "They're curious about the woman who survived a death trap and managed to escape without life threatening injuries, and the woman who managed to steal my heart."

Warmth blossomed in my belly. A sense of safety filled me, but it wasn't a calming feeling. It dawned on me why his friends were there. Like Grady had said, 'they were like family.' The orphanage wasn't a family, but I knew what one was. I didn't have to experience it myself to understand the meaning of it. If these people doubted my strength, I would have to prove them wrong. I wasn't weak. And if this was a test to see if I was good enough for their future heir of Scoria, I could be in trouble. How was one measured as 'good enough?' I glanced at the doorway at the bottom of the steps and felt my fear dissolve. I reached out and squeezed his arm. "I can handle it." Grady's eyes gleamed, a wide grin crossed his face and he pulled me in for a kiss, my knees going weak.

We entered through an arched doorway, and then I stood still, taking in the room. The modest sized rectangular room was the size of a small dining hall lined with carved wooden support beams, the floor was polished ivory granite with swirls of shimmering gold flecks. A large mahogany table sat in the center surrounded by five unfamiliar faces. A fine display of archaic portraits filled the paneled wall beyond the table. A large, wired birdcage dangled in the corner, occupied by two alabaster pigeons nipping away at seeds. *Carrier pigeons*, I thought.

The group stood up from their chairs, swathed with what looked to be some form of ceremonial stole. The navy blue cloth hung below their waist. A maze embroidered 'G' inside what looked like a mountain, rested against their chest—over their hearts.

Two of the men appeared to be in their late fifties, early sixties. Deep furrows bracketed their mouths, and their hair was flecked with gray. The other two couldn't have been much older than Grady or me. The older woman had kind brown eyes. Her brown hair was thickly streaked with gray, and firmly tucked into a knot at the base of her neck. She had a grandmotherly look to her, but yet, one that said she wasn't to be trifled with.

Grady's palm rested low on my back. "This is Rome, and Silas." He gestured to the two older men. Rome's face went pale as if seeing a ghost, unease lined his features. "And these two," he said, pointing to the younger two, "are Brennen, and Wade." They dipped their chins acknowledging me. Wade's clean-cut and lean frame looked out of place next to Brennen. His chest was broad, shoulders thick. Long dread-like spirals pulled back by a leather strip laid across Brennen's collarbone. I had not noticed until then, a green stone fastened to a chain hung around their necks as I skimmed over the men and woman. It mirrored the inlayed stone on Grady's leather bracelet he wore in Ignius.

My gaze went back to the older man, Rome. His luminous gray-green eyes mirrored my own. Grady placed a stiff hand on my arm stealing my attention. He appeared so tense it looked like his muscles would snap any second. Was he worried they were already scrutinizing me?

"Jinx, I would like you to meet my great-aunt. Amani, this is Jinx."

The air whooshed from my lungs. I hadn't been prepared to meet the one woman who stood atop a pedestal in his eyes. She was safe all along. A sense of relief washed over me. Grady no longer had to agonize over her safety. She dipped her chin with a smile and placed her fist over her heart. "Welcome," she said with a kind smile.

"Be seated," Rome said, gesturing to the empty chairs skirting the table. The older man's eyes roamed over my face. An odd expression crossed his. He cleared his throat, turning away and back to Grady. "We were taking a risk leaving the city. As you know, Terrapin has been invaded."

He looked straight at me and I held his stare. He had no clue who I was, yet, he seemed startled to see me. Why had he continued to study me? Quickly I straightened up, giving myself a hard mental shake and slid into the smooth seat. Grady sat beside me and placed a hand on my thigh, giving it a squeeze.

"We will tell you what we can without breaching the Guardian law. But we need your word that what we say stays within the walls of this room. We've gone to great lengths to remain a hidden entity and servants to the greater good of Terrapin and its' people," he said, looking pointedly at me.

They were taking a risk trusting me on whatever it was they knew about this island. I felt a deep sense of gratitude and pride in my chest. I looked from one Guardian to another and squared my shoulders. "You have my word," I stated to them all. Grady smiled with a curt nod. My fingers twined and twisted beneath the table.

Rome cleared his throat. "Let me begin with who we are." He had an heir of supremacy to him, one that demanded my attention, and I couldn't look away. He leaned forward, eyes severe. "We are Guardians of Terrapin, and were born into our positions," he tacked on. "Generations of Guardians have protected Terrapin as a whole and its' secrets for centuries. As such, we monitor specific territories as safety precautions. Whatever happens beyond those is of little interest as our objective is to keep Terrapin from the very hands that could destroy it."

So that was why Grady came to Nordic, I thought. *He wasn't just an heir; he was a Guardian for Terrapin, too.* Why is Terrapin so special?

"As you may have noticed, Terrapin is unlike any other country. We Guardians band together to extract those who pose a greater threat to Terrapin. Lives have been lost..." he said, pausing as if was remembering those taken from them. He cleared his throat again. "And devastation will ensue, but until we work together for a common cause, we lose. The importance of this island's survival and the safety of innocent people depend on it."

The hair on my neck rose and tingles danced along my skin. I'd wished life was less complicated and it was about to get even more. I felt it in my bones and in the pang in my heart. Grady's hand pressed on my leg. I hadn't noticed until then it had been bouncing.

"Jinx."

I was waiting for Rome to continue when Amani pulled my attention to her. My chest tightened. "Yes?" I asked, wondering what she would say or ask. Her tone was firm but gentle.

She brushed her palms across the table as if clearing dust particles away and placed them on her lap. "You now know who we are. We would like to know who you are." She neither smiled nor frowned.

Stark, cold fear ran through me, fear of their disapproval. I felt trapped and overwhelmed as all of them stared expectedly at me. It was another reminder that I was a nobody—an orphaned girl who would be scrutinized for being less than acceptable for Grady. They were different from me. Our skin was the same shade of golden-brown, but they held rank on this forbidden island. And their gazes caused me to sink.

"I can't," I said, feeling the panic rise. I was afraid of what they would think of me. What *Amani* would think of me?

There was a moment of awkwardness, and then Grady said, "It's alright. *I know.*" He looked at me with pleading eyes, willing me to spill my soul to people I had just met and barely knew. It took *years* for me to open up to Casper. And, what did he mean by '*he knew?*' I had never told Grady I grew up in an orphanage or the horrendous things that happened within the fenced-in compound. That was not something I told anyone. Sure, it was a permanent scar on my otherwise clear record, but the only person who knew besides my officers was Casper, and she only knew of the orphanage, not what I had endured while there— not the abuse. I could tell them I was a Nordic fighter pilot, but not where I grew up, because that didn't define the woman I was. Did it? Who we are and who we need to be to survive are two very different things. I wasn't the same girl I was back then.

Amani spoke up. "There isn't anything you could say to wave our opinion of you, dear. What's spoken in this room stays in this room. These are only formalities, you see," she said with a wave of her hand. "We want to get to know you better is all. Do you have a family back in Nordic?"

Family. My heart leapt in my chest. I felt trapped beneath the weight of their eyes boring into me. Acid burned its way up my throat. Discussing my past with anyone was like carving my heart out and handing it over. My words came out bitter. "No, no family. I have no one. I grew up in an orphanage behind a fenced-in yard with boys cruel as poison and my self-worth challenged every single day. Is that what you want to hear? I've overcome my adversities over time and prefer to leave them in the past."

Rome gasped, pushed back his chair abruptly and stood. "Amani, I need to speak to you privately. Please excuse us, we won't be long." He kept his focus on his hands, not looking at anyone except Amani, and then hurried from the room.

I was legitimately sorry for the harshness of my tone and for what I said. With a deep breath, I reminded myself that I couldn't allow my trust issues to make me act or speak irrationally. I had to get a grip and learn to deal with them instead of pushing them away. Some part of me knew I couldn't continue to burry that darkness.

Amani's request asking about my family threw me off. Why would it matter? I hadn't meant to come across defensive, but the subject of my youth was brutally hard to open up about. Grady hadn't seemed at all surprised by my reaction. Why was that? And what was going on with that guy, Rome? From the moment we walked into the room, he appeared perplexed, as if confused by my appearance. His quick glances unsettled me.

"Grady," I whispered. He turned his face toward me, leaning in. The two younger men, Brennen and Wade had spoken in low tones to one another, undoubtedly wondering why Rome suddenly left and glanced in my direction.

"You *knew*?" I said, narrowing my eyes. "How?"

"The night I carried you from the pub in Ignius." He paused. "It slipped out in your drugged state. You have nothing to be ashamed of, Charlotte, you should know that. Actually, I have more respect for you now than ever before." He cupped my cheek in the palm of his hand. "Don't you see? None of that matters to me."

He couldn't possibly have meant that. It was no secret how the Nordic orphanages were ran, and the stories of what went on behind their closed doors. Soon, we would have to have a heart-to-heart. Changing the subject, I asked, "What's up with Rome?"

He shrugged his shoulders. "I don't know. I wondered that myself."

The doors opened up, Amani and Rome went back to their seats, faces neutral. But something told me they were keeping something from us.

"Young lady, we want you to know you have a family, here, with us. I can only imagine the difficulties you have faced and overcome in your lifetime. Know that you have a place in Terrapin—a home. We can always use another strong female Guardian."

Tears rimmed my eyes, my throat thick with emotion. Swallowing a few deep breaths I rasped, "Thank you?" Was she offering me a Guardian position? Going back to Nordic wasn't a possibility, and I knew that, but I hadn't considered where I'd go.

Rome adjusted the cloth around his neck, and then directed his gaze on me. "We believe this group has been building their own army for some time now. With Guardians placed in prime positions, we've been able to collect pertinent information relevant to this claim." He crossed his arms and sat back as he looked around the table. "They're shepherding vulnerable men and children, who in turn, are pledging themselves and services to them."

My lips parted, but I had nothing to say. Could the adopted boys from the orphanages be their recruits? Rucky said he didn't have a choice. Was that what he meant? Did he mean the rebels adopted him? We had to find out who was the mastermind behind their group. If we had a way to get his personal file, then maybe it would lead us to them. Quickly, the pieces began fitting together. This group had been doing the same thing as the Guardians, but instead of protecting whatever value the island had, they were going after it.

"Grady, you once said "what is it you know that makes them want to kill you? It wasn't what *I* knew, it was because I—*we*, the pilots posed a threat to their plans. They were eliminating Nordic's strongest pilots and military assets. It makes sense." I met Silas' eyes. "There's a reason Guardians are protecting Terrapin. Why? What are *you* protecting what the rebel group wants so badly they would *kill* for? If they weaken other countries defenses, that increases their chances significantly for overpowering them. Am I right? And if they succeed in finding whatever it is *you're* protecting, they would be unstoppable." My breaths were coming in rapid succession. I knew I was right, I felt it. They had to see it. "Right?" I repeated, my hands shaking. Rome and Amani shared a look, one I was unsure of.

"She's right," Grady studied the Guardians faces. "The rebels have managed to slip into the shadows and when they strike, it's not all at once. They've been somewhat cunning with their attempts to lessen the governments' strongest defenses. Their temptation has led them to be inept, and evidence has slipped out."

Silas spoke. "You catch on fast, young lady. Grady informed us of the attack en route to Scoria. We are also aware they are seeking you out. They know you survived the air combat and issue a threat of derailing their plans. Their unbridled violence and recklessness to reach their goal has us questioning the size and strength of their militia—and their intelligence. We do have another concern though."

My bottom almost slid from the chairs edge, my body tense. He had my attention.

"The rebel group has managed to get around the island, know crucial locations, take hostages, and we believe someone from Terrapin is aiding their attempts."

Twenty-Two

I overheard Pria tell Grady someone she knew had disappeared. Was she speaking of her half-brother Maru? It made sense. But could her brother be working with the rebels? He could have switched his allegiance from Terrapin to the rebels and no one would know.

"This group is behind the missing and dead pilots in Nordic. Defeating the Nordic government and obtaining control would give them limitless power as Nordic has the strongest military and more land than any other country. Gowen has matched our technology, constructed weapons of mass destruction that could debilitate any countries forces...even Nordic's. Maybe they are Gowen's?"

Amani had remained quiet, and then spoke up. "A man by the name Verek runs an underground black market that's only open to a particular group of people. A few Guardians have trailed him for years. We have reason to believe he's in works with one of Nordics highest advisors, whom is believed to be leading the rebels under the radar. What we don't know is how they managed to learn of the stone."

The *stone*. What did she mean by that? I regarded her curiously. Grady pressed down on my leg again to stop it from busting through the tabletop.

"Terrapin's Heart Stone," she continued, as if reading my thoughts. "Back before any of us walked this planet, the continent shifted, breaking apart land masses and creating shifts below the sea. Terrapin at one time was nothing more than an underwater land mass. Once the shifts took place, Terrapin emerged from the ocean floor, pushing through the water's surface, and over time fortified into what it is now. During the time of its appearance, and before the current state, large masses of webbed feet turtles, also known as Terrapins, made the island their home and nesting grounds. Hence, the name: Terrapin. Brennen, dear, please show Jinx the Tome."

Seconds later, Brennen placed a massive leather-bound book before me. A musty stench wafted in my direction. He flipped the cover over, carefully leafing through the pages, pressing his index finger for guidance. Illustrations of turtles with wing-like legs, beaches, streams and mountains sketched across the pages. The graphic images were precise and clear.

"You see, as the shifts continued, a mass of said turtles were trapped inside the land formation. Over time and through the Seasonal changes, the Terrapins and their eggs had fossilized, creating one massive stone. Our ancestors discovered a rare power within, creating the first family of Guardians to protect it, and a stronghold around it."

There was an underlying significance to her story. Was this the stronghold? The sacred Heart Stone was somewhere within this very mountain? My body buzzed with energy.

"Each Guardian receives a piece of jewelry with a small cut of Heart Stone inserted within, and is marked specific to each Guardian. No two are alike."

I scanned the necks and wrists of the Guardians. Wade's Guardian Stone was tucked beneath his shirt. But the others were visible and upon a closer inspection, tiny divergences with the shapes and sizes were evident. How had I not noticed Grady's but only on a few occasions? And never was it in Nordic. Had he concealed it from prying eyes on purpose?

If only the Guardians carried a piece of the stone, then Rucky wouldn't have had one. I couldn't help but wonder if somehow an undercover Guardian in Nordic had been followed, taken in by the group, or if Rucky had knowledge of it. There were so many variables to the equation, and none of them made sense.

The sketches were beautiful, detailed to the very point. Whoever drew the symbols had a steady, accurate hand.

"Jinx?" Amani's soft voice floated through the room. I pulled my eyes away from the book and met her eyes.

A sudden knock on the door startled me. Rome pushed back from the table, swept across the room and cracked the door minimally, his face obscured by the shadows. Not a word was spoken or the slightest movement noted. It felt odd and awkward as if we were waiting for the key to a major turning point. He pressed the door closed and I followed Rome as he subtly made his way to Amani. He whispered behind a cupped hand into her ear. Her head slightly bobbed but her expression was masked. His movements were nonchalant but stiff. Had something happened?

Amani stole a deep breath and sat in momentary silence. Whatever she was going to say before the interruption was replaced with a closing to the meeting. Wade and Brennen left first, followed by Silas, and then Amani. Rome took the tome, placing it back onto the shelf.

Grady and I were on our way out when Rome spoke to us.

"I'd like to talk to you later this evening." He held my gaze, speaking directly to me.

A sudden chill slid up my spine. I wrapped my hand around Grady's and glanced at Grady for a reaction. He rubbed the back of his neck.

"I'll bring her back in an hour." Grady didn't appear to be affected by Rome's request.

"I'm right here," I said looking between the two of them. I was tired, getting impatient and wanted to spend some time with Casper and hopefully Grady if I could.

"I don't know what you want Rome, but if you want to talk, fine. I'll talk. But I'm warning you…I'm tired—exhausted actually. And a little suffocated by info overload, so if you could make it a quick, get to the point."

He held up his hand, clearly not pleased by my tone. "Get some rest. We'll talk later. He forced a small smile and left.

What the heck just happened? Judging by the look of

annoyance on Grady's face, he didn't know what was going on either, and that bothered me. We walked out the door and up the stairs. He shot me an apologetic look over his shoulder. It wasn't his fault any of this happened. From the moment my feet touched Terrapin's dirt, my system had screamed for normalcy.

We came to a stop by a door, matching the others we had passed. He wrapped his other hand around my free hand, sweeping his thumbs across the top slowly. My heart squeezed at the way his dark eyes roamed over my body. He pulled me into him. Securing my arms around his waist, he pulled back and cracked a half-moon smile that melted my heart. His lips brushed mine, and then pulled me in for a deep, sensual kiss. His hand smoothed my hair aside before gently stroking the nape of my neck. Everything inside me tingled, and craved more of him. "Get some rest. I'll have food sent to your room. I need to find Amani and I'll come back for you."

He gave me one last kiss, turned on his heel, and walked away.

I kicked off my boots, wrapped a small throw around me from the end of the bed, lay back, and dragged my arm over my face, shielding it from the light. Finally, release, as tears trickled beneath my lashes. I couldn't evade the image of my blood coated fingers, or Rucky's scared face as the life went out of him. Overwhelmed and exhausted, I succumbed to the peace and silence. My solitude lasted only moments as a light rap on the door sounded.

"Come in," I said, somewhat annoyed.

"I brought something for you."

Casper. I peered up, untangling the soft blanket from around me.

She ambled over to the bed, the mattress dipped as she sat and pulled her hand from inside her pocket.

My eyes widened at the reddish-brown box in her palm.

"Thought you might want this," she said, extending her hand.

I climbed over to her outstretched hand, taking the tiny box into my own.

"Your bike was too big to sneak out with, and I know this means a lot to you, even though you never talked about it. Nordic officials came not long after your accident. They took everything else; I wasn't letting them take this, too."

I swept her into a tight hug. Wild waves of red hair and the scent of jasmine tickled my nose. "Thank you. But how did you know?" I asked, pulling back to meet her eyes.

She curled a leg up beneath her, tucking a loose strand behind her ear. Her large topaz blues were calming. "I never told you this story, but one night when I came back to the apartment late...really late..." she giggled. "You called it an early night after an intense simulator training. Teeny and I begged you to go out with us...do you remember that?"

It must have been before Commander DeMarco issued early curfews. I shook my head, not recalling that particular evening. Many nights after intense training and hours of mental exertion, I wanted to be alone and pass out.

"You must've been bushed. I found you sound asleep in your uniform with that little box cradled to your chest. I even tried to pry it from your hands, and as soon as I did… it was as if you were guarding it with your life, so I let you be. You, and your box."

I lifted the lid. My stomach knotted tight. The tiny silver locket was still there. Relief washed through me. Twisting around, I held it up for her to see.

"I think this was my mother's," I said, a trace of sadness in my voice. I replayed the day of my given assignment at the orphanage in my mind. The head mistress handed over a small, brown paper bag to my dirty hands, and explained that was the only possession left with me when they found me abandoned on the doorstep. I could remember her bitter tone, the way it stung when she spoke to me as if it was nothing more than a cheap trinket, and I was as worthless as the box itself.

Casper's breath drew in, covering her mouth. She looked at me through sad eyes, and then said, "Maybe she's out there somewhere, Jinx. She must've loved you to leave something behind like that." She peered into the opened palm-sized box, taking in the small locket inside. Casper rarely visited her parents and was an only child. Her father was a crude man, who spent his days deep inside the dirty mines. Her mother worked in the Nordic factories, sewing on machines all day, making uniforms for the military. I'd never cared to meet them, but Casper said deep down beneath their rough exteriors, they had good hearts. She was able to overlook their bitterness and see the positive behind little things they did for her.

I just shrugged my shoulders, not knowing what to say to that. I doubted there would ever be a day I would meet the woman who gave me life. Closing the lid, I slipped off the bed and looked around for a safe spot to store it, my feet spinning me around three-hundred and sixty degrees. The furnishings weren't mine, the room was temporary, and the cave wasn't my home. I spun back around and sat down, placing the box on the nightstand beside the bed.

She patted my leg. "You look like shit. I'm turning in, too." She swept me into a grizzly hug and gave a quick kiss to my forehead. "Karrie mixed some oils to help me sleep. But, I'm in the next room over, not far. If you need anything, you know where to find me."

I sat quietly while I stared at the box still in my palm. Tears burned my eyes, and I looked away before the first one could fall and nodded my head.

Before she was through the door I said, "Thank you." My voice wavered. I swiped my eyes and pulled my knees to my chest.

TWENTY-THREE

My hour was up. Karrie brought a tray covered with an assortment of fruit, cheese and crackers, and set them beside the box on the stand. I had hoped it was Grady. I asked her how Deklan was holding up. By the down turn of her lips and the pinched skin between her brows, I knew his health had deteriorated.

"I don't understand it," She said, pacing the floor. "He was showing significant improvement and even mumbled a few words. It just doesn't make sense."

Her freckled hands ran through her short hair. As she turned for the next lap, I spotted a leather band around her wrist—her Guardian Heart Stone. Two sterling ovals surrounded the brown-green stone and set on a dark brown leather band, not any wider than a pinky finger.

Suddenly, my breath hitched and my pulse began to

hammer. Perspiration formed along my palms and I whipped my head back to the little box on the stand. *No. It couldn't be. The locket.*

The door clicked into place and Karrie was gone. It was just me, my thoughts and the box. I scrambled up from the bed, kneeling down in front of the nightstand as if I were sending a silent prayer. My shaky fingertips gently slid the box closer to the edge, willing me to open it as if it silently spoke to me. Placing my trembling fingers on the lid, I raised it up. The little locket gleamed at me as if winking, prodding me on. Taking the locket into my fingers, I unclasped the locket anxiously. I'd always held the key and never knew it.

My heart dropped. It was not there, the sliver of stone; the exact stone set within bracelets and leather bands the Guardians wore. Nausea set in. I shook my head, "no." The brownish-green, thin stone was gone. It was gone. I flipped it back and forth, as if it would appear or as if my eyes played a sick joke on me. Then, I grabbed the box only to find it empty save for the burgundy liner inside. My head swam with a torpedo of dark thoughts. My knees trembled, ready to give out, and then crumpled beneath me. The box rolled from my dead fingertips to the ground. *No.* Even in my head, it sounded like a weak, raspy whisper. *Breathe*, I told myself.

Grady. I had to find, Grady. I grasped the locket firmly in my palm and tore from the room. *Which way do I go? Where would he be?* Lit sconces lined the wall; their orange-yellow glow flickered, casting ghostly halos across the stone ceiling. My heartbeat accelerated with intensity and excitement. I peeled off to the left, checking each door one after the other.

As I pushed the millionth door opened, my breath hitched. "What are you doing?" I demanded, as a startled Pria withdrew a needle quickly from Deklans' limp arm. Her head whipped to the side, jaw dropping in surprise. The needle slipped from her grasp, shock evident on her face.

"It's not what you think," she rushed to say, but I saw it in her eyes.

It was *exactly* what I thought. She was trying to kill Deklan. But why?

She recovered the needle and rushed toward me. Quickly, spinning around; I slammed the door in her face, holding onto the doorknob with everything in me. My chest clenched tight, squeezing the air from my lungs. I shoved the locket into my bra and braced my feet on either side of the door for leverage, my fingers slick with sweat. Readjusting my grip, I was losing my hold.

Pria pounded on the door, and pulled on the handle as if it was a game of tug-of-war. "Listen to me you nosey bitch, you have it all wrong." The door bobbed back and forth, never latching as both sides fought relentlessly to gain the upper hand.

"You're a sociopath—you're a liar! You set us up. It was you the whole time," I grunted out. Sweat beads formed along my hairline. My jaw clenched tight. *Where was everyone? Grady should've been here by now.*

Pria was strong. Our battle remained even. She was as stubborn as I was.

"Is your situation so dire you'd murder your friends? Give

up, Pria. I'm not letting you out." Grunts came from the other side of the door.

"You should've stayed out of this. Now you don't have a choice. You'll regret this," Pria said harshly.

"The only regret I have was feeling any sympathy for you. You don't deserve sympathy, you deserve another black eye, bitch."

Sweat trickled down between my shoulders and back, bleeding through the thin cotton shirt. Readjusting my footing, I pulled harder against the doors knob. She jerked the door with a powerful thrust, enough to slip and wedge her boot into the small space.

"Damn it." Adrenaline still pumped through my veins, but my fingers were slick with sweat, and they were slipping. *Don't let go.*

A sharp pain pierced my hand. "Ouch," I said breathlessly. The needles shiny exterior gleamed in the flickering light. My grasp slipped away, the momentum throwing me hard against the stone wall. My legs folded in and I sank down to the floor. Before I could shake off the fall, Pria was on top of me, needle in her hand.

She had a feral look on her face. I wouldn't give up. I bucked beneath her, trying to throw her off, but her legs squeezed my sides. Our arms were struggling to pin the others' down—a fierce struggle between right and wrong. She was strong, stronger than I'd thought.

She bent over, our faces merely inches apart, staring down in pure malice. "Stop fighting me," she said in a low, ominous voice.

"There's a special place in hell for women like you, Pria. Women who are self-serving. Women who's jealously eats away integrity and honor. What you've done is unforgiveable," I rasped. Without thought, I thrust my head forward, smacking hard against her lips with a crunching *thunk*. She screamed out in pain and disgust. Ribbons of blood poured from her mouth and nose, covering the bottom half of her face. A metallic tang pierced my senses. Thick crimson rained down on me, rolling over my cheek and down my neck. The reality of her injury sank in, looking at me in horror. It worked. Taking advantage, my arm broke loose and connected with her jaw.

My head whirled, and smoky patches distorted my vision. Grabbing Pria's arm and pushing her off, I rolled to the side, stumbling to get up and fell back onto my knees. She quickly recovered. A sickening sensation slithered through my belly as I caught her steely stare and face coated with thick red blood and the needle still in her grasp. I blinked my eyes, but the black spots only seemed to widen and my heart seemed to slow despite the adrenaline. Pria stiffened. Footsteps pounded our way. She lunged forward, the tiny needle coming at me like a silver, shiny bullet.

My arms and legs betrayed me. I could barely breathe. I was numb. With a sinking feeling I acknowledged she was going to kill me, too. Her head shot up, a look of surprise and confusion crossed her face. Recognition. A gust of air whipped past me as two bodies crashed into Pria, and then complete darkness swallowed me whole.

TWENTY-FOUR

"It's been two days. Shouldn't she have woken up by now?" Worry laced with something else was evident in the quiet whispers. Soft footsteps of pacing feet filled the air.

"She's been through a lot. We don't know how much was injected into her system. She's young and strong. Vitals have improved and..."

"Get it out of her. Make her tell us. I don't care if we have to get it by force. I'll slit her throat myself if I have to."

I knew that deep voice, his deep, wonderful voice. *Grady.* He was evidently pissed about something. Whose throat was he going to slit?

"I'm going to talk to her. Keep me posted on Jinx's status. She'll pull through, man. I've seen the determination in that woman's eyes. She wouldn't go down without a damn good fight." Seconds later a door latch clicked into place. Even through the foggy haze, I recognized the accented voice. Luke. No. He wouldn't be here.

Blue sparkling lights twinkled like stars in the Nordic sky on a cloudless night. I blinked away the ghostly haze from my eyes feeling the flutter of my lashes against my skin. In a chair across from the foot of the bed, Grady was hunched with elbows on his knees and his hands planted in his hair. I could remember the issued shorter haircut on him, but this newer grown out version was incredibly sexy. He untangled his hands and ran them down his face. He looked sad. Or was he frustrated? Clasping his hands, his swept up eyes met mine and froze.

I gave him a lazy smile. He sprang from the chair and was at my side in a heartbeat. His handsome face was level with mine as he knelt on his knees.

"Hey, you. Who's got your boxers all bound up?" My throat was dry and scratchy and my breath left much to be desired, but I didn't care. Though he seemed unsure, he flashed that dimpled smile I loved more than anything.

"We'll talk about that later." He turned away a moment. By the rise and fall of his chest, I gathered he was collecting himself. "Damn it, Jinx. I was so worried about you. You frighten me sometimes, and exhilarate me, and challenge me to feel things I never could—see a possibility of a future I'd never considered." His hand gently smoothed my hair aside before he pressed his forehead against mine. "I'm never letting you out of my sight again." His breath was warm and smelled of mint.

"Then don't," I whispered, wanting him to press his lips to mine. My body buzzed with desire at his words, filling my tummy with warmth and butterflies. The urge to run my fingers through his hair was strong. When I start to raise my arm, a strange tug on my skin stopped me.

A deeper voice came from the side of the room. "You're attached to an IV. I wouldn't move your arm around, you're liable to pull it right out. I'll get Karrie and have her secure it and add some tubing to lengthen the line."

Rome pulled the door open and paused not looking back. "I'm glad you're okay." With that, he disappeared behind the door.

Rome had heard the intimate conversation between Grady and I, and my cheeks warmed from embarrassment. "I didn't see him. How long had he been in here? How long have I?"

His silky chocolate eyes searched mine. Raising my non-IV'd arm, I cupped his face in my hand. Days of stubble tickled my palm. "Tell me what happened."

He released a heavy breath. "Pria...she...the needle had poison in it. Rome and another Guardian saved your life. If they hadn't been close by...I'm so sorry I wasn't there for you, Jinx." Unshed tears pooled in his eyes. My heart thundered in response. I hated seeing him so torn up over something he had no control over.

Then out of nowhere I blurted, "Charlotte. My name is Charlotte."

"*Charlotte*," he repeated slowly. Somewhere between lust and intimacy, sharing my true name with him felt completely right. My heart surged with an unexpected joy and a newfound liberation. And I wanted more.

"Charlotte." I couldn't contain my smile. He leaned in stealing a supple kiss. Pulling back, he laced his fingers into mine, thumbing soothing circles. "You couldn't have known what she was planning. Please don't beat yourself up over this, okay? I feel fine, good, actually. I remember what happened, Grady—all of it." My heart did a one-eighty degree turn from calm and relaxed, to a pulse-pounding thump. "Pria killed Deklan. I saw her pull a needle from his arm…"

"Shhh…slow down." His head bobbed up and down. "I know. Rome and I detained her and she admitted what she did. She also admitted to drugging you in Ignius." He ran a hand down his face, a pained expression evident beneath his hooded eyes. Pria was a childhood friend and regardless what she did, it had to sting all the same. He trusted her. "She will never be able to hurt you or anyone ever again. There are a few Guardians interrogating her now. I should probably be there, but I don't want to leave you."

My thoughts circled back to the night at the brew house, to the image of the dark haired girl slipping into the shadows behind the bar. "I'm fine, truly. Go, get out of here." I flipped my wrist toward the door. "Go torture someone else for a while," I teased, hoping to lighten the mood.

The uncertainty of why Pria killed Deklan still remained. How could she take the life of a friend? Close friends or not, ending someone's life before their time…was it possible Pria was in works with the rebels? I would have to talk to Grady about it. He stood, placed his forehead against mine. "I'll send someone to guard your room while I'm away. Try to stay out of trouble." He snickered, then placed a kiss on my forhead.

"Grady?"

"Yeah?"

"Don't forget we have plans tonight."

Suddenly his body went stiff. With a pained expression he said, "That was two days ago. But I promise I'll make it up to you. My days are yours…my nights, too. I'm all yours." With a kiss that made my toes curl, he spun on his heel and left.

I'm yours, too.

TWENTY-FIVE

Two days and nights lost to the darkness of poison. How close had I really come to losing my life? Grady didn't have to tell me, but I knew Deklan was gone... dead. If only I had found his room sooner, maybe he'd still be alive. A steady flow of guilt grew, not understanding why anyone would intentionally kill another. Then, I remembered the sucking sound as the knife broke through Rucky's abdomen and forced higher by my hand. The blood glittered darkly, black as oil in the semidarkness. A shiver ran through me. *It wasn't intentional*, I told myself.

I looked down at the plastic tube taped to my skin and wondered if Karrie put it there. Her freckled fingers were gentle with Deklan. A light tap rapped on the door. It must be the guard Grady sent.

"Come in," I said, still a little nervous.

Rome stepped in, shoulders stiff, but he didn't look away. Instead, he headed toward me, his forehead creased like I was a puzzle that needed solving. As he drew closer, I lifted my chin, bracing myself for a second inspection like he had in the Guardian's chambers. My stomach churned but I didn't move. No matter how uncomfortable I felt from his prying eyes, I held his stare. He no longer wore the Guardian garb, but a charcoal gray sweater that pronounced the vivid color of his eyes. Pulling the chair away from the wall, he angled it to have access to the door and me.

"I believe you dropped this," he said as he withdrew his hand from inside his pocket. Resting in the palm of his outstretched hand was my locket. It must have slipped from my bra in the struggle. And until now, I had forgotten about it. The look on Rome's face said he was pleased with his find.

Forgetting, I reached out for the locket and recoiled, feeling a sharp pain when the IV catheter pulled hard against my skin. "Ouch."

Rome leaned forward placing the little locket on my lap. The shining silver was so pretty against the royal blue down comforter. "Thank you."

He seemed pleased with himself as his lips pulled up, but immediately dropped. What could have changed his emotion so quickly? We sat in silence, and eventually, he cleared his throat. "You look so much like her."

I glanced at Rome, but his eyes are fixed on the locket as if speaking to it. "Like who? I asked, confused and curious, and wondered if that's why he looked at me strangely.

"Yamila. At first when I saw you I thought I was looking at a ghost. The resemblance is uncanny, really." He smiled then. Creases lined his mouth from age. He shifted in the chair, clasping his hands.

"I'm sorry. Was Yamila a friend of yours?" I asked, not quit understanding where the conversation was going.

"No...and, yes. She was my daughter." He looked up. Tears threatening to spill down his cheeks. "And that locket..." He pointed to the silver trinket on my lap. "That was hers."

I squeezed my eyes closed. A lump formed in my throat. I tried to push it down, but it wasn't going anywhere. Finally, after a moment, I looked through blurry eyes at the locket. *Could it be true?* The *want* to believe him was so strong it hurt. With a heavy heart, I lifted the locket into my hand. The feeling was all-too familiar.

"How can you be so sure? It's a simple locket. Anyone could replicate it." Why would he think this specific one was hers? There had to be an unlimited supply of these simple charms. If he was trying to persuade me to give it to him, he would be disappointed. It was mine.

The bed dipped below his weight as he perched his hip on the edge. "May I?" he asked hesitantly. Flecks of gold were noticeable in his gray-green eyes. They were shockingly similar to my own, but I brushed it off as a coincidence and nodded.

He took the locket into his thick fingers. He was gentle with it. "You see there?" He pointed to the circular lip, hidden beneath was a flat button no larger than a tip of a pen. Pressing against the tiny spot, the back opened a sliver. He said nothing of the missing stone, yet he knew of this secret button. He pulled the silver backing to the side. A folded piece of ivory paper fluttered to the blue comforter.

Ignoring the paper, he faced the backside so I could see it. My eyes narrowed, studying engraved initials: YCS. I was having trouble breathing. I locked my arms to keep myself upright. Beside me, Rome's face paled. I shared a glance with him and he nodded. "Yamila Charlotte Sloan."

He hadn't looked at the backside right then, but he knew the exact initials and their order. His daughter's middle name… what did that mean?

He placed a steady hand on my back. I leaned into him and drew strength from his touch. A steady stream of tears dripped onto the comforter, turning it to a darker shade of blue. We sat silently for a few moments, not knowing what to say. Finally, I took in the enormity of it all, cleared my throat and said, "My birth name is Charlotte." A flood of tears broke loose as the words slipped from my quivering lips.

I often wondered if the orphanage mistresses issued names for me and the other orphans, at least the babies. My eyelids drifted closed as I drew in a deep, quiet breath, and pulled myself upright.

"I don't know what's come over me," I said, wiping away the tears. "I'm not a crier…well, I wasn't one, let's put it that way." I sniffled. These surprises had to stop.

Rome had obviously been crying, too, as his eyes were red-rimmed and puffy. "You'll have to excuse me," he said, wiping a hankie beneath his nose, "It's just unbelievable. All these years…I never knew…" Pinching the bridge between his eyes he whispered, "She did it."

What did he mean? Did Rome know she was pregnant? My head swam with 'what ifs,' and 'whys.' I needed him to say it out loud, tell me what we obviously already knew was the truth so I could move on to the 'accepting phase' of this revelation. A myriad of questions streamed through my mind, but most importantly what happened to Yamila and why she abandoned me. Distracted by reflection and emotion, I had forgotten about the little note on my lap. I took one last brush under my eye and picked up the folded paper. Wondering what it was, I unfolded it cautiously to avoid tearing it, one side at a time.

I analyzed the inky drawing of two Guardian symbols and just beneath them, '*CHARLOTTE*' was written. But, inside the *O*, was a purple arrow pointing to the first *T*, and the *L* was crossed off in red ink.

The mattress jostled as Rome stood up, straightening his jacket and tucking the hankie inside the breast pocket. The red hue of emotion that circled his eyes had dulled to a light pink. The stern demeanor I had seen in the Guardian meeting was no longer evident as he smiled down at me. "I'll give you some time alone to be with your thoughts. I'll be right outside the door if you need anything."

He stepped to turn, but I stopped him. "Rome? Would you like to hang out with me for a while?" To my astonishment, I could see that he actually wanted to stay. He hesitated by the chair a moment. I patted the spot beside me and scooted over, leaving room for him to settle in beside me, breathing in a scent of aftershave and a woodsy musk. There was light behind his smile. He took the offer and there we were, two strangers brought together by fate.

We talked easily for hours, and I would have never guessed that we could become close so quickly. I listened intently as Rome shared his memories of Yamila as a child and as she grew into a young woman. We laughed and shared tears. I'd never grow too tired or bored with them. It seemed Yamila and I had similarities and resembled each other in so many ways—her stubborn determination to prove herself, her need for space…I could identify with those. He told of dreams and fears as she became a young Guardian. And because Rome's wife passed away after giving birth to Yamila, she was his world.

I envied her and the life she lived, her freedom to explore, and the look of pride her father had in his eyes as he spoke of her. Though, nothing was as complete as when he wrapped me into his arms and called me *Granddaughter*.

That night, I laid in bed thinking about the woman who gave me life, about how different it would have been had she been in it. Would she have braided my hair, taught me to write my name and tuck me into bed? Would she have warded off the monsters I feared at night? Tucking the soft comforter beneath my chin, a ribbon of sadness clenched my heart.

Rome quickly fell into his paternal role, not allowing anyone under any circumstances to visit me, saying I needed some space and rest. I almost argued with him, but thought better as I took comfort in his protectiveness, and I was actually sleepy. I closed my eyes tightly, willing myself to sleep. The sooner I did, the sooner I could see Grady and tell him.

Throughout the night I heard the door hinges squeak. Every time I cracked an eye lid open, it had been Rome checking in on me. He quickly became my favorite person and I giggled to myself at the cuteness of his actions.

Rolling onto my side, my eyes settled on the locket. I still was uncertain what the note meant, but I decided to wait until morning before showing Rome. Perhaps my reasons were selfish, but the note was meant for me, and it had been hidden for eighteen years. A few more hours wouldn't change anything.

TWENTY-SIX

I awoke to muffled arguments beyond the door. Arching my back, I raised my arms to stretch, but hesitated. I peered up at the damn tube taped to my hand, but it was gone. Blinking a few times to clear the sleep from my eyes, I pulled myself up, staring around groggily. "I have a grandfather." *I have a grandfather.* Letting that sink in, I reached for the locket and stopped. Not only was the locket there, but it was placed on a fine rope of leather. And, behind the necklace, a framed picture of a smiling young lady tucked under Rome's arm. Her russet layered hair was swept to the side, familiar gray-green eyes lit up by what appeared to be happiness as she smiled up at her father. *Yamila, my mother.* The resemblance was remarkable.

I slipped the necklace over my head, suddenly feeling loss and love. I'd lost out on a relationship with her, but perhaps it was the only way to show me she cared. Now that I'd found the note inside the locket, I couldn't wait to see what the code meant—and discover the secret she left behind. I stroked my fingers over the smooth silver. Even if it wasn't a clue about where my mom may have hidden or a trail to lead me to Rome, it was still a piece of her, and I wanted to know what happened to her. First thing first, it was time to show Rome.

Someone turned the knob on the door before I called out. My heart leapt with joy as Grady walked in. Tossing back the covers, I leapt from the bed and into his arms. By now, he was sure to have heard Rome was my grandfather.

"Finally," he whispered, his voice slightly choked with emotion, with relief. "Rome wouldn't allow anyone in...not even me."

My heart rose up in my chest. Grady grinned at me, and I smiled, too. His close proximity sent my heart into crazy palpitations. "I have so much to tell you." I was nearly bursting at the seams to tell him everything.

He touched my face wordlessly—this time with the back of his steady hand, stroking once from my temple to my jaw—before he stole my lips with his. But he seemed pained when he placed his forehead to mine, like he wanted to say something but held back.

"What is it?" I whispered to him. "Is something wrong?"

"It's nothing. I'm just glad you're okay."

He was lying to me and I wanted to know why. Pressing him wouldn't get me anywhere so I changed the subject. But inside, my chest tightened with concern.

Is Rome outside?"

He nodded. "He's still out there," he whispered.

"He needs to see something," I replied, reaching for the locket resting against my chest.

Grady stared at me for one short moment, and then turned toward to door. "Rome," he shouted, startling me.

The door swung open. A serious look on his face. "Is something wrong?" His concern was adorable.

"Look at this," I said, unlatching the back compartment, catching the paper in my palm. I tried to focus but it was hard with Grady so close. Taking a step back, I handed Rome the little paper, hoping he would be able to decipher the code from Yamila. "This was inside the back panel."

Grady sidled up beside us. "What is that?"

"Exactly," I said, unsure if Rome would understand the script either. "Clearly it's my name, but why the arrow and the X? What does it mean?"

He blinked, his forehead creasing as if he'd been stumped. Before he could answer a thought came to mind.

"Do you think she was pointing out the 'T' for Terrapin?" It seemed too obvious, but I looked at him expectantly, as if to confirm my finding. If that was true, how had she expected me to figure out it stood for Terrapin when it was geographically impossible to find on any map?

"Possible," Rome said. He took it from me and held it to his face.

How many times had I wondered if our paths would cross? And I was completely unaware the answer to finding her was held inside the locket she left me—that is, *if* she was alive. I shook my head, trying to reassemble my now confused thoughts. Rome said Yamila was a Guardian, but never where or what happened while she was there.

Grady breathed out a sigh, loud enough for me to hear. He'd shifted, and his face was turned toward the door. Rome, on the other hand, looked encouraged.

Casper burst through the door, Brennen right behind her.

I didn't turn around. The paper was a magnet, and I was drawn to it.

"I don't want to fight with you Rome, but you can't keep me from seeing my friend any longer," Casper said, her hand on her hip.

"Casper." Brennen's voice was a command. "I tried to stop her, sir." He looked at Rome tensely.

Rome's brow creased angrily for a moment, then smoothed as his eyes took on a knowing look. "It's okay, Brennen. She's fine here with us."

"And you thought you could stop me, Dreadlocks." She smirked then winked. "But maybe you should stick around. I'm feeling a bit mischievous today," she said pulling up beside Rome, looking over his shoulder.

It was silent for a moment, only inhale and exhales of breaths audible. As I examined the red X, I frowned to myself, unable to make sense of it.

"Look at that." Casper interrupted my thoughts, pointing at the X. "X marks the spot."

I stared at her for a long moment in astonishment.

"What?" She was too observant sometimes. "Is something

wrong?" she asked in a low voice. "You seem…anxious."

"That's it! Casper you're a genius!"

I could tell she was confused. Her meaningless chatter deciphered a piece to the puzzle none of us could figure out. I stared down, concentrating on Yamila's scrawl. *X marks the spot.* But, why the *L*?

My stomach twisted nervously as I considered various possibilities. It could easily be a person or place. Place… I hesitated for a moment, as if I wasn't sure my theory was correct. Then I released the breath I was holding and said, "Lucia?"

Rome turned to stare at me. He gazed into my eyes without speaking, his eyebrows furrowed in concentration. I stared at his face, waiting for confirmation.

"Unbelievable."

I closed my eyes and took a deep breath. I had to find out what Rome knew or any details to sum up my burning questions. Was she alive or not?

I hadn't told Grady, but his unsurprised reaction meant that Rome informed him. I was braced for him to tell me it was ridiculous, but clearly he understood what I was thinking and agreed.

My heart pounded painfully. The significance to the puzzle was a map leading me to her—my mother. My conscience told me so. And if Yamila was alive, I had to find her. I *had* to.

I WASN'T PAYING much attention to my surroundings as I exited the bathroom. I hadn't showered in days and I felt utterly disgusting. Straightening the whitish-gray fur vest and double-checking the dark belt I successfully wove beneath the pants leather straps, I still couldn't get used to not wearing a uniform. Grady managed to unearth a pair of combat boots my size, which I was eternally grateful for. I ditched the others without hesitation.

I rounded the corner and smacked straight into something hard. "Oh."

Grady had stood silently by the door, waiting for me. He still wasn't the same Grady I'd known before yesterday. And somewhere in a corner of my mind, I felt bad about it.

His eyes appraised me, taking in the damp hair, leather pants, snug sweater, and back to my eyes. He raised one eyebrow and let out a low whistle. "That was made for you."

I smirked. *There* was the Grady I knew.

"No, I meant it's a perfect fit. Just right."

"Thanks," I scoffed, giving him a hard time.

He lifted my chin, studying my face. He bent his face slowly to mine, pressing his lips to mine. "Mmmmmm…," he moaned. His nose gliding to the corner of my jaw. "You drive me crazy."

I never imagined I'd ever find someone I wanted to be with so badly. I could feel his warm breath on my neck, feel his skin on mine.

"I know you're still recovering, but can we talk?" he asked, brushing my hair back with his fingers.

Shivers danced along my spine. He could have whatever he wanted when he kissed me like that. I hadn't noticed the heavy coat on him until then. I realized it had been days since I breathed fresh air. I smiled. "Of course." Taking my hand, he led me to the end of the hallway, through a steel door, up a staircase, and at the end of another hallway was a metal ladder attached to the stone wall. Above the ladder was a trapdoor.

"Here. You'll need this to cover your wet hair." He offered a circular fur hat with matching flaps on the sides that hung below my jaw.

"What is this?" I asked, as I carefully climbed each rung, following closely behind him. Grady unlatched a lock, and pushed the panel up and over. His hand reached down to me from the opening. Clasping his hand, he pulled me over the lip and onto a blanket of snow. I gasped.

"This is where I come when I need clarity and privacy."

I understood why. The city of Scoria was spread out below us, the seasonal change settling in close to the shore. A spectrum of light appeared in the sky, arching over land and water. A hazy multicolored arc rimmed on the outside—red, violet—on the inside. White capped waves crashed against the rocky shore, and shot up into the air.

Even though it was almost noon, the wind swept by, chilling me to the bone.

"Here." Grady pulled his arms from his coat, wrapping it around my shoulders.

"It's like the edge of the world. It's beautiful up here." I sighed, soaking in the view.

I tore my eyes from the scene and turned to see Grady standing behind me, gazing out at the sea.

"So what did you want to talk about?" I asked, curious. Concern flicked across his face. "What's wrong, Grady?" I asked, and reached out to take his hand and pulled him closer. "Is it the rebels? Have they done something?"

He was silent a moment, his face unreadable. "No. Quite the opposite actually. They've been pulling out of Terrapin for several days now. The Guardian Council concluded they weren't equipped to handle the Seasonal Change. There's no guarantee they've all left though. We haven't been successful extracting anymore information out of Pria and the blizzard made it impossible to travel out. Weather conditions are worse in higher altitudes, but you already know that."

My eyes shot wide. "That's great news they're pulling out … so, why aren't you smiling?" My nervous stomach coiled tight. My throat constricted.

His expression was a strange mix of frustration and defiance. He exhaled, squeezed his eyes shut, then looked me straight in the eyes. My heart pounded almost painfully.

"Charlotte..," he paused, "I've never talked about this before…"

I cupped his cheek in my hand, gliding my thumb over his temple. I could feel how tense he was against me. I wanted to hear what was tearing him up, erase the internal turmoil from him.

"When I was eight, my parents set sail on their twelfth anniversary. It was supposed to be a celebration of life and their commitment to one another. Work was never far from my father's thoughts, always mixing business with pleasure. 'Light two candles with one flame,' he'd say. After years of trying to get pregnant for a second child, my parents found out they were expecting right before they were to leave. She convinced my dad she felt well enough, not wanting to disappoint him," he said softly.

"I was young. My juvenile mind comprehended desertion, not as going on a short retreat. I begged them to stay, used my childhood charm, stomped my feet—but to no avail, their minds hadn't changed. During a tantrum, I told them I hated them." He released a huff of air, evident the reeling memory became vivid and real all over again. "Their lives were dedicated to Terrapin and its people, but most importantly to me...or so I thought until then."

My heart bled for Grady. In the orphanage, a parental bond was only a dream, an intangible, but for Grady, he had that. He had two people who loved him and cared for him. But I sensed bitterness in his tone.

"My mother, Helene, swayed my father to shorten the voyage due to my pleading. She had a weakness for me, promising it would only be for one week then they'd be back. By the time they were due to port, my anger turned to excitement. I remember waiting on the docks in pouring down rain for their ship to sail into port..." He shook his head, released a heavy sigh.

"See there?" He took my hand in his, guided me a few feet from the ledge. Snow crunched beneath our boots, the cold wind pricked at my skin. A steep embankment ran down to another ledge, littered with sharp stones, snow, and a broken tree branch. Far, far below where the sand met the sea, was a small harbor. The same harbor where a young boy, long ago, forced by tragedy, became a man.

"We were told a fierce storm capsized their boat, and any vestiges were swallowed by the sea, never to be seen again. I've made my peace with it. I do have one regret, one I'll never make again. I was a kid and couldn't have anticipated they wouldn't return. Regardless how angry I am, I'll never part with someone I love without telling them just that. I just wished I had the wisdom to tell them that then."

He was holding onto a promise he'd made from pure heartbreak. I pulled him into my arms and cradled him to me. "I'm so sorry, Grady," I whispered to him with equal quiet. There wasn't anything I could say to mitigate the painful memories. I just held him close.

Moments later, he pulled back, and locked in each other's gaze. He choked on his words. "What I'm trying to say is that since their death, I've never loved another the way I loved them. They were taken from me and a part of me died inside that day. It wasn't until two days ago I was reminded of that deep feeling of love and loss again and it scared the hell out of me."

My thumb traced over his cheek. My words caught in my throat. This beautiful man standing before me had spilled his soul, shared the darkest most intimate memory in his existence and I stood there unable to comprehend the depth of his pain. I have never loved anyone, so I had no one I loved to lose. But if it was anything resembling the look on his face, what it did to me, I understood more than I thought. Behind the composure was a man who knew the value of life and would never take it lightly.

"Thank you."

His brows pinched together. "For what?"

"Bringing me here, sharing with me…"

"Don't thank me, Charlotte. To better understand me, you needed to know. I wanted you to know."

I rolled up on my toes, wrapped my arms around his neck, and kissed him. The chilled, smooth lips of his mouth sent a wave of fire through me. He tightened his arms around my ribs, deepening our kiss. Inhaling the scent of wood smoke and leather, I felt at home in his arms.

Grady brought his head close, resting his forehead on mine; blonde-brown waves fell around my face, soft against my temples. My chest rose and fell as I drew in a breath.

"Please don't ever leave me," he said faintly, and I was unsure I heard correctly. "You're freezing. Let's get you inside before Rome turns the place upside down looking for you." He smiled and his lips found mine again.

TWENTY-SEVEN

Yamila was on my mind. All I wanted now was the truth. Was she gone forever or was she somewhere out there waiting, hoping one day her daughter would discover the clue and come find her?

When we entered the living room, the hearth's light reflected by the windows, flickered across the walls. Falling snow emerged beyond the windows. Winter had laced the glass with frost. But something caught my eye. I would have recognized her anywhere, and her red hair gleamed under the funneled light—Casper. Relaxed on the couch, she laughed at something someone said. As we neared, wound around her finger was a thick strand of Brennen's spiraling dreadlocks. He closed his eyes and leaned back against her legs. Apparently she wasn't joking, she was feeling mischievous.

My stomach grumbled as I inhaled the aroma of something

wonderful in the air. Pots clanked and steam hovered above a sizzling pan on the stove. Karrie pulled a craft from an overhead cabinet, and sprinkled flakes of something into the skillet beside the pan.

In Nordic, meals were only offered four times a day and if you missed your meal, you dealt with the consequences—hunger and loss of personal wages as our meal cards were funded through our own accounts. The chow hall was always jam-packed. Never once had I prepared a meal with my own hands.

Grady must have sensed my curiosity and said, "Most likely, Karrie could use some help."

With a nudge, I broke away and started for the kitchen and felt Grady on my heels. I bit my lip to hide my smile. Pulling up beside Karrie, I offered my assistance, though, I knew nothing about cooking. She was all too pleased to let me help. We immediately began working alongside of her—stirring, blending and mixing concoctions.

There was a frenetic vibe in the air. Casper and Brennen seated themselves at the table with a deck of cards and instantly the chairs filled as new faces and ones I'd recognized joined the game. Shouts and laughter rang out and my heart swelled with happiness. For now I was safe. And the people I'd grown to care for were safe, too.

Grady departed saying three was a crowd, but I knew he itched to get in on the games. After a few rounds of cards, Grady, Wade, and Brennen disappeared. They came back, each adding a leaf to the table, extending the length fit for an army.

"Thanks for allowing me to help, although I didn't really do much besides add a mess," I said to Karrie, giggling as I gazed over the splattered cake batter and back to the dripping beater in my hand.

"A few lessons with me, girl, you'll be a pro. Besides, what fun is cooking for rowdy men if you don't have entertainment while doing it? You did great."

Karrie and I made a quick sweep of the kitchen, wiping down counters and putting away ingredients. She must have noticed the confused look on my face after glancing at the crowd. "The shorter blonde is Kamy—lots of energy, but fun to be around. There—," she jabbed a finger across the table, "—her name is MaKenzi. Don't let her petite frame throw you off. She's one of our best fighters. We dubbed her 'little mighty.' Their Guardian training is almost complete. We expect good things to come of them. They're fearless."

I liked that—'little mighty.' They looked to be in their early to mid-teens. "How old are they? I asked. Karrie handed over thick mitten-like things. I wasn't sure what to do with them, still curious about the two baby-faced Guardians.

"Place those over your hands. They'll protect your skin from being burnt pulling out dishes from the oven. The girls are roughly twelve and fourteen I'd say."

I conceded and slipped them on. They felt odd, not fitting snuggly to my hands like typical gloves. Three others entered the frenzy around the table swathed in a combination of fur and leather. Flecks of powdery white snow covered their shoulders and crown of their hats.

"And they are?" I asked, tipping my head toward the new arrivals.

"Ah, the one on the left, the tallest, is Grail. Brennen and Grail are brothers. That one in the middle, her name is Brandie. She's Grail's sexpot."

I shot Karrie a questioning look. "A wha…"

She snickered. "They're lovers. Just ignore them as best you can. They can't keep their hands off each other. It's disgusting, really." Her tone hinted she was joking, but I began to wonder just how much PDA I'd be witness to tonight. Brandie's hands were already busy, buried beneath Grail's fur coat. Wisps of short dark brown hair peaked out from beneath her hat. Blue eyes the color of a midnight sky sparkled beneath long dark lashes as she winked up at Grail. I tore my gaze away and back to Karrie and began counting the blanket of freckles across her nose as she introduced the final of the three.

"And that one," she said, pointing to the man withdrawing arms from the coat. "His name is Theo. If you don't want to know a truth, don't ask him. He was born without a filter." We both laughed. I often thought my filter was fractured. Moments later I pondered that thought and decided my filter wasn't cracked. I just told the blatant truth.

"Then I better stay away from him." I laughed.

Grady pulled a chair out, placed a soft kiss to my temple and motioned me to sit. My heart fluttered at his touch. His affections weren't as subtle as they once were. There was an unexplainable force that made me gravitate toward him, but I was no longer scared of my feelings and drew comfort from his touch.

MaKenzi caught my eye as Grady slid the chair out for me. A devilish grin spread across her face. "Grady and Charlotte kissing in a tree. K-I-S-S-I-N-G. First comes love, then…."

"Then, comes your ass-whipping if you don't shut up," Grady interrupted. Laughter spread throughout the room.

Theo piped up. "I'm never getting married. Women are crazy."

"*You're* crazy, Theo. And an idiot. " Brandie added. "What about you, Brennen?" Brandie's eyebrows bobbed up and down.

"Oh yeah, I'll get married," he replied.

Brandie's smile widened. "And what will she look like?"

Brennen leaned back in his chair, arms crossed. Clearly, he was thinking it over. He scratched his chin and smiled. "She'll be a feisty redhead who's not afraid to pull my chains," he said, yanking on a dreadlock with raised brows.

Casper's face was as pink as a flower.

As the table was set and seats filled with bodies, a sudden sensation of dread came over me, one I couldn't displace. I picked at the food with my fork, surprised my appetite had vanished.

Introductions to the Guardians, as well as small chatter, were seamless and fluid. The younger two, Kamy and MaKenzi spoke animatedly about their earlier training and how Theo was being a real tool, assuming it was the same Theo who sat two chairs down from them. I could relate. Many of my trainers were a-holes and intentional jerks. But all the while as I nodded and smiled, I couldn't ignore the clawing ache. It ate me up inside and left me hollow. Finally, I understood. I found myself imagining a life with Yamila over and over; so much so, that the burning desire to search for her trumped everything else, especially the dinner.

I whispered into Grady's ear, explaining there was something I had to take care of and would catch up with him later. I excused myself from the table, reassured Grady everything was fine, and steered away from the frenzy. Once I was out of sight, I made a beeline down the hall in search of Rome. And I had a feeling I knew right where to find him.

When I reached the familiar double doors to the Guardian chambers, I stopped to pull in a deep breath of air, dropping my gaze to the iron knob. I placed my palm on the iron, wrapping my fingers around the chilled knob. My desire to learn the truth was so strong it was almost a physical pain. I knew what I had to do.

I pushed through the door into the Guardian's chambers, half expecting no one to be there. I came to an abrupt stop, my heart clenched inside my rib cage. To my surprise and relief, I recognized the older man hovered over an aged book. Rome.

"Charlotte." Rome looked at me speculatively over wire-rimmed glasses that hung low on his nose. "What brings you away from your friends? Shouldn't you be eating dinner?"

Keeping tabs on me? How cute. "We need to talk." I tried to hide my restlessness and speak casually. He looked at me blankly. "I'm not subjecting you to verbal release therapy. That's what girlfriends are for." He sighed with relief. "Pull your boxers up grandpa, this may take a while." He chuckled, pulled the glasses from his face and set them on the table. It was nice he had a sense of humor. I had always hidden my emotions from others with sharp talk and bold gestures. Rome had known me only for a short while and as his granddaughter even less, which was hard for my quizzical mind to grasp, but he no longer looked at me as a stranger, only someone he respected.

He gently closed the book, slid it aside and gave me his undivided attention. "As I suspected, with time you'd come seeking answers. Am I correct?"

Taking in the lines of his face, I nodded. "Yes. It's time you leveled with me, Rome. Not just about Yamila, but about everything."

"No matter what I tell you, the future is unpredictable."

"I'm good with unpredictable."

"Yes, yes you are," he replied.

I pressed the door mostly closed and walked around the square table.

"Take a seat." His arm swept out, gesturing me to pick any chair. Pulling out the closest seat to me, I settled against the wooden back and fixed my gaze on Rome.

"Is she alive?" The words burst from my lips. I was prepared for him to tell me no, but I wished more than anything he'd say yes. My head and heart were at odds.

He shook his head. "I don't know." He sighed, and then ran a hand down his face.

All my hopes evaporated—my half-formed plan to leave Terrapin, to set out in search for my mother, even finding the person responsible for my intended death—the uncertainty

held me back from making an informed decision about my
future. Before I could ask him what he meant, he started in
again.

"Time plays tricks on the aging mind. For nineteen years
I believed, hoped she'd find a way back, but the not knowing
nearly did me in, Charlotte. Her letters stopped coming and not
a day has gone by that I haven't thought about her." His posture
turned in, shoulders hunched.

It was clear to me how much he cared for his daughter, the
tone in which he spoke nearly undid me. Easily, I could have
gone to comfort him, but my body remained frozen, unable to
move.

He cleared his throat and met my gaze. "You've held the key
to our questions the whole time." A smile turned up his lips.
"Miracles weren't something I believed in…until that locket fell
into my hands."

I reached my hand up, running my fingers across the
smooth, silver locket secured around my neck. "Until you found
my locket?" I asked confused, glancing down as if the answer
was etched into the smooth metal. Perhaps his aging mind
was playing tricks on him again; there was nothing unusual or
altered that I could tell.

"The note, Charlotte. It's in the note." His eye grew as he
leaned in, a flare of excitement in his voice. "If our suspicions
are correct and the circled L is in fact a clue, then Yamila may
still be alive."

My hand shot up stopping him. "Wait. Something's missing
here. Why would her letters just stop? Was she in danger? Why

does the note make you think she's alive? And why would she abandon her child?" Heat trailed through my body and down my limbs. I'd pulled the sensitive subject out from beneath the darkened hole I'd buried in my mind.

"Your mother was a special woman. She was my daughter and I loved her more than she knew, more than anything. But as a Guardian, we all are sent on tasks to secure the safety and protection of Terrapin, regardless of who we are or what position we hold..."

"Like Grady." It was a statement, not a question. Grady had explained why he was in Nordic, though I still was thrown as to why they would risk sending Scoria's only heir for a job another Guardian was capable of.

"Yamila was sent to the Palin region of Gowen, not far from the Nordic/Gowen border. During her service, a man entered into her life. Unfortunately, she allowed him into her heart, too. You see," he said, resting his clasped hands on the table. "Rarely do we send women into the field. Not because of their gender," he clarified, "but it takes a trained mind, someone who can separate themselves from any emotional bond and stay focused on the task at hand."

Karrie was a Guardian. Thinking back on my interactions with her on base, she was all business, a dedicated worker who wasn't out frequenting the pubs, or traipsing around with boyfriends. What Rome explained made sense, so why, if Yamila had feelings for this guy, did she drop off the face of the planet?

"I can sympathize with what you're saying, but why wasn't she ordered to come home? Why did she stay?"

His head bowed and he staggered on his words. "It was too late. I'm afraid she was ashamed of her predicament and would figure out a solution on her own without reaching out. Yamila realized too late he wasn't what he seemed—while already pregnant with you and close to term, he became extremely possessive. She was alone, frightened if she attempted to leave he'd come after her. He strangled her carefree nature. And he was well aware of her pregnancy. Hiding you was her only option. So she did, she hid you. She found a way to save you. Yamila knew he'd kill her if she fled and she couldn't bear to leave her baby under his influence."

"You knew about this and you just left us there?" I said bitterly. My pulse was going too fast, and my head felt dizzy. Frustration welled in my chest with every passing second. I looked away and swore a shadow lurched from the doorway. Alarmed, I narrowed my eyes, but the shadow was gone. I turned back to him.

For one long moment, Rome just stared down at his empty hands.

"By the time the letter reached me, it was too late. As you know, Terrapin is void of technology. I would've rescued her had I known. She was in more danger than we knew." His voice hitched. Sadness etched his eyes. "My dear, that's why no one was able to find you. She was gone and no way of knowing if indeed he'd taken her life…" He swallowed. "Or if she escaped. Until you pulled the note out of the locket, we assumed she was dead. That note proves she made it out alive."

"What about the man?" I couldn't bare saying father or dad,

because that man was neither to me.

"He too, had disappeared. We've never stopped searching for them. It wasn't until about ten years ago his location was detected in the trifecta where Gowen, Lucia, and Nordic join. We assume his location meant he'd been in and out of all three countries, which was why he was so difficult to locate. His home is more of a fortress, surrounded by men who work for him. "

"But…" My efforts to speak were cut short.

"Hear me out, Charlotte. That man is dangerous and whatever is running through that thick skull of yours, don't under any circumstances, entertain the idea of seeking him out. Guardians have gone above and beyond—tracking him, digging up information on him, and nothing moral comes back."

The hair on my neck prickled as I let his words sink in. I'd always teetered a fine line, was I the balance between yin and yang? Half good, half bad? I wondered if he had a family and was trapped like Yamila once was.

"She's alive. I can feel it. Maybe it's instinct, I don't know, but regardless, I have to find her. I *need* to find her…and I need your help, Rome. Out of respect, I am begging you. Please help me."

Silence.

If Rome could secure an aircraft or boat, get me to Lucia, there wasn't a piece of land I wouldn't traipse or turn over to find her. "Please." Suddenly, the spacious room seemed small as if the walls were caving in on me, extracting the very air I breathed from my lungs.

"I want to find Yamila as badly as you do. Your survival is evidence enough for me to believe she's alive, but the fact still remains, rebels roam this island, and I couldn't live with myself if something happened to you."

I pushed away from the table and stood, anger surged through my veins. "I'm very well aware of the situation and I'm also aware their efforts were cut short by Seasonal Change, lessoning the risk of attack. Cut and dye my hair, send a few Guardians with me if that's what it takes. I don't care."

I could tell he was contemplating as he began picking at the skin around his nails. Finally, after minutes of deliberation, Rome circled the table to stand beside me.

"Okay," he whispered, almost as if defeated. "I'll make the arrangements."

The urge to wrap my arms around him was strong. Instead, I smiled a heartfelt smile and said, "Thank you." Those words seemed inadequate, a contrast to the feelings coursing through me. I was going to find my mother. How was I going to break the news to Grady?

Sensing my hesitation, Rome swept me into a tight hug. When he pulled back, his hands cupped my shoulders, his gray-green eyes held mine. "With the Rebels on the island, many of our Guardians are busy elsewhere. Fortunately, for us, the ones I'd choose are here. Brennen, Theo, Brandie, and Grail will assist you on your journey. I trust them with your life." He paused.

"I'll call a meeting first thing in the morning to secure the plans with the Elders and the Guardians. Get some rest. You'll leave the evening after next." Placing a gentle kiss on my temple, Rome disappear into the halls shadows.

"Thank you," I whispered.

TWENTY-EIGHT

ounting glowing blue stones peppered across the ceiling as if they were jumping sheep didn't help my restlessness. Sleep wouldn't come easy. In less than forty-eight hours, I'd be on a ship or an airplane, sailing across the Grand Rouche in search of a woman I hoped to call mother. My stomach coiled into firm knots as my thoughts shifted back to Grady. I practiced, recited many ways to convey the news to him, but they were as ridiculous as counting sheep.

"If she's alive, she can be found. Where are you Yamila?" With a sigh, I peeled back the thick comforter. Chilled air swept across my exposed skin, sending a wave of prickles down my skin. With slow movements, I swung my legs over the bedside, and slid my bare feet onto the plush rug below.

The cave was eerily quiet and still, the only sound was my shuffling feet as I worked my way toward the chair in the corner.

My cargo pants, sweater, and boots still lay where I left them, limply across the chairs arm. As quietly as I could, I slipped the sleeper gown over my head and quickly pulled on my pants and sweater feeling instant relief from the cool temperature.

Lacing boot strings in the faint glow of the stones proved a difficult task, but one I accomplished after a few measly attempts. I pulled my hair up into a bun with the elastic band around my wrist and moved to the door. The hallway was tinged with a sliver of light that funneled through the living rooms large windows and into the hall. I reached out and placed a hand against the bumpy stone wall to anchor myself, and crept forward down the tunnel of stone as the light dissipated to shadows.

My palms were clammy, but I kept them skimming across the rough wall to guide me. I should have lit a candle or dug around for a damn flashlight. Lurking through the halls like some sort of creeper in the night wasn't the smartest decision I've made. *Crack.* "Ouch. Damn that hurt," I berated myself as I rubbed my banged up forehead. And there was the corner I'd been waiting for.

Eventually, I traced the path Grady had taken me down toward the ladder where the hatch waited above. Remembering the bitter cold from my last jaunt on the mountain top, I extended my arm around as if blind, searching for the mounted coat hooks.

"Aha, found you."

To my relief a heavy coat hung from the hook as well as the fur hat I'd worn. Slipping my arms into the coat and the hat on my head, I started for the latch at the top, one rung at a time. I made my way through the hatch and carefully replaced it.

The night's frigid air bit my skin and stung my nose. I wrapped my arms around myself and looked up soaking up the view. The hemispherical arc of the moon shone brilliantly against the deep palette of night. This was Grady's Senders Rock.

I sat on a blanket of snow admiring the view and allowed myself to relax without thinking. Breathing in calm and exhaling nerves.

Metal clinking pulled me from my daze. My head whipped to the side as the hatch door flipped over and a mop of brownish-blond hair popped out. "Mind if I join you?" His lips pulled up on one side deepening the sexy dimple above it.

"Of course," I replied, patting the snow beside me. Footsteps crunched over the snow as he moved toward me. Using his hands, he lowered himself slowly behind me. There wasn't an inch of space between our bodies.

"Here, lean back. I've got you." The deep timber of his voice stirred wild flutters in my stomach. My back pressed up against his firm stomach. His thick arms circled around my shoulders, cradling me against him. His head dipped against my cheek, his mouth against my ear and whispered, "Couldn't sleep either, huh?"

I shook my head. "No, I couldn't sleep. I'm sorry I didn't come back. I…"

He placed a finger on my lips. "Shhh…you don't owe me an explanation. But you do still owe me that date."

I could feel the skin on his cheek pull up and I knew he had that sexy smirk on his face. Just the thought undid me. Heat surged through my body, reacting to his every touch. I leaned to the side and pressed my lips against his, breathing in his woodsy scent. His fingers tightened around my waist and rose up to my shoulders, then slid across my neck to my jaw. The kiss deepened and I buzzed with lust.

I nipped his lip with my teeth playfully.

"Hey," he said, his voice was rough and raw. "I never pegged you as a biter." His laugh shook our bodies. I needed that. I needed him, this moment alone where we were the only two in the world.

I lifted my head and stared into those bold brown eyes. "Grady, I need to tell you something." I was afraid. But I had to tell him before we lost ourselves completely. "You told me there was no one else I could trust more and I trust you'll support me when I tell you this."

His brows pinched and tipped his head back, studying me.

"I'm your friend; you're my number one concern. You can tell me anything. Always."

My head jerked back. "Friend?"

"Er…Best friend?"

"No, I already have one of those."

He scratched his chin. "Boyfriend? Because if you don't have one of those, I'd gladly fill that spot."

I looked up in astonishment. "Boyfriend. I'll consider it." The mood was flirty and light, but I had a ten-ton brick pressing down on my chest and I had to suck it up and get it over with.

"Grady, I'm leaving in a few nights to look for my mother."

His body tensed beneath me.

Silence.

"Please don't look at me like that." My stomach dropped. "Come with me. Help me. I want you with me," I said with pleading eyes.

His mouth opened, but nothing came out. "Why now, Jinx?"

My heart dropped to the soles of my feet, if that was possible. How could I explain to the only person who's ever given a damn about me, I was about to leave him? I'd never imagined a life with a parent, any family for that matter, and now I had a chance at finding her, I didn't want to waste another day or week or month.

"Because my heart," I placed my palm over his heart. "And my head." I placed a soft kiss to his temple. "Are aching. I wasn't expecting this, but fate dropped me a line, and I'd be a fool to let it go. I thought you, more than anyone, would understand. Hoped, rather."

"I don't know what to say. I'm shocked, angry, hurt, sad, and...damn it, Jinx." He dropped his head back avoiding me with a growl.

Then I remembered his faint words I'd barely heard the last time we were up on this rock, '*don't ever leave me.*' I pulled at his chin. I needed him to look into my eyes and when I was satisfied I said, "Hey, I'm not leaving *you*, Grady. I'm not leaving *you*."

In one fast motion, he swept me into his arms and buried his face in my neck. My heartstrings tugged in every direction.

"Rome called a meeting for first thing in the morning." His

body went stiff. My tone was soft but comforting. "His plan is to send Grail, Brandie, Theo, and Brennen with me. But Grady, you have to know there's no one in the world I'd rather have by my side than you." My teeth chattered.

He pulled back and kissed me deeply, fervently. There was so much emotion I was almost drowning in it. We pulled apart, our chests heaving for air. He placed his forehead against mine while sweeping slow strokes with his thumb across my jaw and said, "Stay with me tonight. Let me hold you in my arms."

"There isn't anywhere I'd rather be."

GRADY'S ROOM WAS similar to mine except for the laundry strewn across the floor and a mounted weapons armoire beside a massive bookcase that stretched from ceiling to floor. Situated above the wrought-iron headboard, hung a poster of a jet in flight. It was an exact replica of the A-80 we flew in Nordic, except mine was rusting at the bottom of the Rouche. The bedding was turned back and rumpled, revealing brown sheets beneath the comforter.

"Watch your step. Sorry about the mess."

"I should go change." As I turned to leave, his hand wrapped around my waist pulling me into him. My hands shot up resting against his chest. "Or not?" I rasped.

"I've got you covered."

Damn him and that smile! All I could muster was a weak nod. Would we really get any sleep? I couldn't help but wonder.

Grady pulled a t-shirt from a chest of drawers on the opposite side of the room. Thankful for the cute undies Casper brought me, I breathed a sigh of relief.

Grady was too much. He offered to turn around while I changed. It wasn't necessary as he'd seen me in a towel dripping wet in Ignius. The T-shirt was thin but soft. I slipped it on over my head then made a mad dash for the bed. I was able to slip beneath the covers before he had a chance to peek. Of course, the air was chilly, which didn't help my "girls" from standing at attention.

He flipped the light switch down and so went the lights. A labyrinth of glowing stones etched the ceiling casting a halo of blue around the room. I scooted backwards, my eyes locked on his face, making room for him. The mattress sank with his weight as he slid beneath the covers and closed the distance between us. It felt natural, not awkward or uncomfortable. I curled into him, feeling every dip and mound.

"Tomorrow when the Elders and Guardians meet, I'm going to ask for their approval to go with you," he whispered. "You've got a crater sized target on your back."

"A crater? That's all? The one thing I'm good at, I'm failing miserably." My penchant for pissing the wrong people off grew considerably since surviving the accident.

He shook his head exasperated. "This isn't a joke, Jinx. Those men mean business and if they are willing to kill to get what they want, I know the Seasonal Change isn't going to run them off. They want you *and* the Heart Stone, and they want it bad. I'd feel much better if I was with you, protecting you."

Those words struck a chord. I didn't need protecting. I'd gladly have him by my side but I didn't want or need a babysitter. We were more than that.

"I don't need to be protected all the time. It's not the relationship I want, Grady." I rolled over to face him.

He propped himself up on an elbow and met my gaze. There was a sadness etched into his eyes that weakened my spirit. His hand rested on the dip between my hip and ribs, his thumb tracing a pattern over my covered skin. Shocking heat surged through me.

"I know you want to find your mom. But I'm not okay with you risking your life to do it."

Regardless of his pleading, my decision—one I'd thought over through and through—had been decided. There was no polite way to tell him my mind was made up. I just hoped that he would find it in his heart to forgive me and to have faith that everything would work out.

"You've made your point. It is a risk, I agree. But I'm not going alone. Theo, Brandie, Grail, and Brennan will be with me. Rome said he trusted them with his life, and I'm confident I'll find her if she's out there somewhere. If I don't go, I'll never know...and it will kill me."

Silence.

"Don't try to stop me, Grady. I'll resent you for the rest of my life. Just let it go. Please."

Grady, who looked like he had just been drug from a torture chamber, released a heavy breath and fell back onto the bed, draping an arm across his face.

When I'm sure he'd given up, I whisper, "I'm sorry."

How had we gone from one extreme to the other so quickly? I hoped that he, more than anyone, would understand.

"I can't just drop it, Charlotte. Just think about it…for me."

I bit my lip, glaring up at the constellations of glowing stones. I felt him turn over on the bed we shared, blocking me out. I rolled over, too, with a heart heavier than lead. The rest of the night was quiet. We didn't talk, or make-out. At some point throughout the night, my eyes grew heavy and welcomed the sleep.

TWENTY-NINE

"Morning, beautiful."

I whipped the covers up over my head. "Noooo. Five more minutes," I rasped, tucking the comforter tightly around me.

"We have a meeting in…mmmm…twenty minutes."

I sprang up from the bed, tossing the blanket halfway on the floor. "Why didn't you wake me up?" I gathered up my clothes, nearly tripping over a pant leg and ran to the door.

"Aren't you forgetting something?"

"Damn you and that dimple." I raced across the room to Grady as he leaned his back against the dresser, arms crossed, smirking. I pecked his lips, spun on my heel and sprang from the room. "Nice legs!" I raised my middle finger as I tore around the corner. His laugh echoed down the hall as if mocking me… and my bare legs.

"Shit," I said, suddenly aware of what I was wearing and how exposed I was. Brown strands fell from the loose bun as it bobbed, smacking against my neck.

Quickly tossing the pile of clothes to the floor, I pulled open a drawer to grab a few essentials: a pair of cargo pants, a long-sleeved Henley, woolen socks, and unfortunate looking pair of underwear. I spun around looking for my boots and realized I left them in Grady's room. I'd get them later. My stomach grumbled as I rushed down the hall to the bathroom, the scent of cooked bacon floating through the air.

I flipped the bathroom light on, discharged the T-shirt and hopped into the shower in record time, no time to enjoy it.

After I was dressed and blew my hair dry, I picked up the dirty T-shirt, tossed it into the hamper, and headed back to Grady's room to retrieve my boots. In the distance, four silhouettes emerged, haloed in the mornings light. Grail, Brandie, Theo and Brennen. They were already on their way to the meeting.

"Crap."

"Ah, morning, Charlotte." It was Brennen's voice.

"Good morning." I turned into Grady's room to avoid conversation and hoped they didn't notice my bare feet.

"Looking for these?" My boots dangled in Grady's grasp like a kid teasing a child.

"Give me those," I swiped at the boots, but he jerked them higher into the air. "Quit toying with me. Give'em here." I jumped again and again without success.

"Only if you say the magic word."

I stomped my foot, fists on hips. "Now." I tried to maintain a steady glare, but I went weak and gave in, switching tactics. "Pretty please?" I batted my eyelashes.

He swept me into his arms, capturing my eyes with his. His tongue ran over his lips so I leaned up, wrapping my arms firmly around his neck and pulled him into me, stealing a deep kiss. "Can I have them now?" One brow pulled up and I tilted my head.

"You can have whatever you'd like if you keep kissing me like that." I smacked his stomach and stole my boots from his grasp.

Did that mean he forgave me? "Sucker." I couldn't help but smile smugly. "Grail, Brandie, Theo, and Brennen passed me in the hallway on my way in here." I pulled the boots on and tied them up. My nerves began to slither into my stomach. "Ready," I said, straightening my shirt.

"Hey, Jinx?"

"Yeah?"

"I'm sorry about last night. I don't want to pressure you or try to change your mind about waiting to leave. If it were me, I'd feel the same way. I respect whatever it is you decide to do."

I bit my bottom lip. My chin dropped to my chest and I pretended to be very interested in the cuff of my sleeve. When had I become so selfish and self-centered?

"I'll wait for you," I said softly. "I can hold out a little longer if that's what you need. I'll do that for you. Rome won't mind, I'm sure."

His warm hands cupped my cheeks and he pulled his

forehead to mine, eyes closed. "Thank you."

Grady and I had laced our fingers together as we wove our way to the Guardian's Chambers. Unconsciously, my hand drew up to feel my mother's locket, pulling comfort and assurance from it. This meeting wasn't the typical gathering. I'd sat through maybe hundreds of briefings, but none of them compared to this one. I released a heavy breath as we approached the double doors.

"If you don't want to go in, you don't have to," Grady said softly, probably sensing my hesitation.

I wanted to come. Now that I was standing there, I wasn't so sure. I drew back to look him in the face. "A few old Guardians don't scare me. Their decision on whether or not you can go does." I put on a smile for show, but deep down I was a nervous wreck. He had only been back to Terrapin for a short time, and I was concerned with the Rebel threats and the islander's unease, they'd make him stay. I wanted Grady with me when I left Terrapin. He calmed me, made me feel safe, and his kisses were out-of-this-world.

Guardians and Elders gathered around the enormous wooden table, talking among themselves. As I settled into the seat Grady pulled out, I didn't miss the dark look Silus casted my way.

Amani had been absent since my first encounter with her on my arrival. Her mousy gray hair, twisted neatly into a bun, rested at the nap of her neck. Her skin appeared gray and her age lines appeared more profound than before.

"Shall we get started?" Her voice came out frail but gentle.

Amani nodded at Rome, who took over. He cleared his throat. "Now that we have everyone here, let's begin. As you are all aware, a recent inexplicable discovery has led my granddaughter, Charlotte, to me."

I blinked, taken aback by Rome's bluntness. Everyone's eyes had fixed on me. In that moment, I wanted to curl into myself and hide my face behind Grady.

"We have evidence to believe my daughter, Yamila, whom we assumed was dead, may in fact still be alive. Where, you might ask? Evidence points to Lucia. I've discussed with Charlotte in length whether or not searching for Yamila would be a double-edged sword. Lucia is a large country and there would be a lot of ground to cover. In addition, up to this point, have not unveiled the identity of the individual behind her attempted assassination…" He paused, adjusted his collar. "But I can't deny this woman, my granddaughter, her right to look for her mother, and more so, finding my daughter. Now, Brennen, Brandie, Grail, and Theo…" he addressed the Guardians, gazing at each as he said their names, "you will be assisting Charlotte on this expedition.

I thought they would protest, insist the idea was ludicrous, but they dipped their chin, accepting the request.

Rome placed a silk map across the table, smoothing out the folded lines. The map pictured the countries Prave, Lucia, Gowen, Nordic, and Senna. And far off into the blue of the Grand Rouche, was Terrapin. Below the dot signifying Terrapin, was a blown up carbon copy of the island.

"There's still a threat of the rebels on the island, so to

secure safe passage to the docks a group of Guardians will set off first to scout the area. The Phantom pulled into port recently. Therefore, will need a day or two to restock, refuel, and guarantee the vessel is secured and ready for Charlotte and the others. It will leave port immediately upon boarding. I'm confident the people will mostly be settled into their homes by nightfall so passage through town should be uneventful."

My heart pounded as I listened to Rome going over details. I tried to focus and pay attention, soak everything into my memory. The boat would only take us to a specific longitude/latitude. Going any further would be problematic, as technology would detect our presence. From there, a large raft would be unloaded, and my group of Guardians and myself would change course toward Senna.

Once there, we'd travel the outskirts of the fishing village, Dune, to the next town north, Marguerite. Rome's contacts, Crystal and Drake, would provide us a place to rest and supply fake identifications for each of us.

Rome addressed Grail, Brennen and Theo specifically. "Only Brandie and Charlotte are to approach them." His tone was stern. He slid his hand into his pocket, pulling out what appeared to be a rock, but with veins of the Heart Stone within it.

"Show them this." He handed the stone over to Brandie for safekeeping. "They will supply you with a vehicle to take to the Senna/Lucian border. And getting over the Senna/Lucian border could potentially be difficult. Hence, the I.D.'s. But I have faith you'll cross without any complications. Their military is small and austere. Once into Lucia, it's all up to you."

Grady shot me a quick glance and his gaze went back to Rome. "I want to go with them." His voice was sure and confident. "It's no secret that Jinx...*Charlotte* has always been fiercely independent. But when her life spiraled out of control, she'd opened herself up enough to trust me. She needs me now more than ever, and I'm not going to sit back and watch her sail away with men she doesn't know—who don't know her...or her mood swings," Grady said, his voice stony but calm, facing the Elders.

I blinked, caught momentarily off guard. Grady gave me a sheepish grin and whispered, "Calm down, your leg is bouncing."

"Are you saying you don't trust your men...or her? She's an adult, Grady. And you have an obligation to your people. We all know the precarious state Terrapin is in. The people need your assurance they are safe—that there's nothing to fear. We don't know if the Rebels have all left or are hiding. You leaving while our people are vulnerable will cause an uprising!" Silus' fist slammed down on the table. He shook with anger and a vein bulged from his neck. "We're in the middle of a crisis!"

"Listen," Grady said exasperated, pinching the bridge of his nose. "My presence in Terrapin will change nothing. Amani still holds the title. And as far as I'm concerned, me being here and not with Charlotte would tear me apart."

"What are you saying? You feel responsible for her?" Rome piped up, placing laced fingers on the table. I could hear curiosity behind his words.

Grady directed his eyes at Rome, a determined look on his face. "No. You should and for her safety. And we both know no one would protect her like I would. No one. And that's why I should go with them."

"This is blasphemy!" Silus cut in.

"Is it? Have you never considered what this must be like for her? Did you or did you not defy the Guardian Law when you procreated with a woman from Prave, produced a child, then sent provisions to see she was taken care of? She's had no one to take care of her, and I'll be damned if I sit back and listen to you preach about *my* responsibilities."

Color drained from Silus' face. He drew in a deep breath, shocked.

Grady leaned back, arms crossed. "What? You didn't think I would be privy to this information, *Silus*?

In one quick sudden movement, the older man's chair screeched across the stone floor as he pushed himself away from the table and blasted Grady with a foreboding glare. "How dare you compare my life to yours! I'm not the heir, you are!" His voice raised an octave as he pointed a shaking finger at Grady.

"Exactly. And I'll make my own choices. And yes, she's an adult, but there are men out there who want to take her life. And I'll personally see to it that her future includes breathing."

"Sit down, Silus. Remember your place," Rome cut in, breaking the tension. I mentally cheered him on.

Silus regained a sliver of composure, complying, then settled back into his seat. He clenched his jaw, his stare pierced through me. The last thing I needed was to gain another enemy.

But why he hated me, I was unsure.

"A child with blood of two races wouldn't have a home in Terrapin. And I knew that. I did what needed to be done."

Intuitive and fearless, Grady stood, capturing everyone's attention. "She means more to me than you know, and I will not apologize for that. Her home is here on Terrapin, with us, Silus."

Grady turned to face me. "Let's go. I'm done here." He took my hand and led me out the door without a backward glance, where it went silent to deafeningly loud. As soon as the door shut, Grady's stiff pose relaxed. He wrapped his arms around me and buried his face in my hair.

"Are you okay?" I murmured, wrapping my arms around him. I didn't think Grady anticipated an argument from the Guardians on whether he could or couldn't leave Terrapin. And, Silus' resistance bothered me, but I wouldn't let his ignorance derail my plans. Whether or not Grady was by my side, my mind had been made up. As soon as I found Yamila, we'd come straight back to Terrapin. In Grady's arms was where I belonged, and as long as his duties resided in Terrapin, that's where I wanted to be.

"No. I'm pissed."

I worried Grady's reaction to Silus would prompt the other Guardians to reconsider. Regardless, Grady and I had to return to the meeting. Leaving abruptly on loose terms would only cause a setback, and fester an already sensitive matter.

"We have to return to the meeting, Grady. As much as I don't want to, we need to."

He gripped my hands firmly, placing a kiss below my ear.

"Why should I?"

I raised an eyebrow at him. "How about because you don't have a choice. You're a leader, Grady. Stomping off because you're angry makes you look weak. Don't let Silus get under your skin."

"You're right." He ran a hand down the back of his neck.

We entered back into the chamber. Grady apologized for losing his temper, but refused to look at Silus. Signs of tension dissolved and the meeting continued.

Somewhere in my deep subconscious, I knew Grady would have to stay in Terrapin. It was the right thing to do. My heart volleyed in my chest as the Guardians made their final decision.

The meeting had been adjourned, and the Guardians and Elders were distracted by conversation. The mood was a mixture of unspoken thoughts, tensions and concern. Forty-eight hours was all I had left to convince Grady how incredible he was and I intended to spend them showing him.

Loud footsteps pound down the hall. A quick succession of rapid knocks blasted against the door. He didn't wait for anyone to reply or open it. Luke burst in and shouts, "Pria's gone!"

THIRTY

The small group sprang to life. Chaos erupted and shouts rang out. But I was frozen in place, unable to complete a coherent thought. Pria was on the loose and Luke, my captor, barely stood ten paces away.

"Charlotte, the boat will leave tonight. Do you hear me?" My shoulders shook beneath Rome's grasp. "Charlotte. Do you understand me?"

Instead of nodding and smiling, I looked into his familiar eyes blankly. It was all too soon. There was supposed to be more time. More time with Grady, Rome, and Casper.

"Grady, take her to pack. Don't leave her side for a second. Go. Now. I'll meet you and the others by the hearth in thirty minutes."

Before I could do or say anything, my body was being pulled from the room and Grady and I were sprinting down the hallway. Feet pounded behind us, the familiar sound of urgency. Men and women I had never seen before littered the halls, some were barking orders, and others were searching rooms like a colony of ants fleeing their hole.

We peeled around the corner and into my bedroom. Without thinking, I spun around grasping his arm, feeling the blood beneath my chilled fingers. "What just happened back there? And I'm not talking about Pria."

He hesitated, like he didn't want to tell me, like I'd fall apart. The next words were like a knife to my heart. Grady drew in a deep breath and somehow I already knew what he was going to say.

"Luke is a Guardian." His voice cracked.

The air was knocked from my lungs. Then suddenly, it all made sense. Grady knew Luke, not just as a childhood friend, but as a fellow Guardian. His mouth opened, about to give me a thousand reasons why he never told me. Instead, he heaves a sigh. I could see the desperation on his face.

"I was going to tell you. But—"

Instantly, memories fell into place and I threw up my hand to stop him. "He said he recognized my flight suite...said he knew where I was from. Over and over he asked if I was alone or if there were others. Luke knew you were in Nordic, and he was worried you were in the battle, too, wasn't he? Worried his friend was shot down." It took all the restrain I had to keep from pounding my fist against his chest. But something tugged at me, holding me back.

A long beat of silence expanded through the room. His

hands found my wrists, pulling me to him. "You're right." He wraps me in his arms, hugging me, holding me tight. "Now you know everything. I'm sorry."

Did I? Did I truly know everything? His eyes were half-open when I pulled back.

"I swear I wasn't keeping this from you on purpose." Grady placed his forehead against mine. "I didn't get the chance to tell you. There are so many things I wanted to share with you from the beginning…but I couldn't. Not then. Luke's a great guy. He would've never laid a finger on you, Charlotte. He knew Pria was up to something, he had to pretend to be on her side."

"It's okay, Grady. I get it," I whispered, feeling a strange sort of calm come over me. My tone must've convinced him I meant it because his expression softened.

What concerned me the most was that Pria was no longer behind bars or a locked door. I could only pray the Guardians would find her and detain her once again. I longed for those forty-eight hours to prepare myself and say goodbye. My time was out.

"I need to grab something from my room. There's a duffle bag beneath the bed. Pack whatever you can and quickly. I'll be right back." He kissed my cheek and disappeared behind the door.

THIRTY-ONE

My brain ran with fury, mulling over every detail, every location, then Grady entered into the room and my brain quit working. It went blank, but my hearts flutter took over, compelling me into his arms. As he intended, no doubt, I forgot all about my worries, and concentrated on the man before me. His lips met mine, warm and gentle, until I wrapped my arms around his neck and threw myself into the kiss.

He raised his face; it was serious. "You still have twenty minutes to change your mind." He raised his hand to my hair, carefully brushed it across my face, tucking the strands behind my ear. His face was tight as he explained. "Wait. Wait a few weeks for things to settle down here. Let me assure my people. Give me time." His jaw hardened. "Please."

I wanted to lean in, to inhale the scent of him. I pushed the feelings aside. My decision was made. Wasting time agonizing over the outcome—the Elder's decision, would do no good.

"I have to find her."

He turned, staring down at me.

"You would do anything to find Amani—put her life before yours, bargain with the enemy, leave Terrapin if you had to—if it meant saving her. If my mother is alive and in danger, you can't ask me to stay."

He regarded me with moist eyes, the expression of sadness on his face. "And, if the choice was between finding your mother or saving your own life, what would you choose? Are you willing to risk yourself—us, on a chance?" I could see the fight going out of his eyes.

The answer was obvious to me. I nodded slowly. "Yes."

He turned is face away. Gently, I gripped his chin, forcing his eyes back to mine and away from dark thoughts. "Why are you doing this to me?"

Tears welled up, blurring my vision. His fingers came up and gently brushed a tear from my cheek, then swept me into a tight embrace. "Because I love you," he rasped.

Hot tears burned my eyes—the burning truth at the tip of my tongue. Did I have the strength to say those virtuous words? "I..." I swallowed, opening myself up to him in a way I never had to another, "I love you, too, Grady." I wasn't too wounded or fragile. My heart swelled as if it would explode. True to his words, never again would he allow hurt or anger hold him back from saying what he felt. *He loved me.*

A smooth surface touched the tips of my fingers as Grady

slid something into my hand. I looked down at the small embroidered square—*his* call sign. My brows pinched.

"What's this for," I questioned.

"I want you to know you have something to come back to."

My body went still as his large hand circled my own in an intimate hold. His body angled toward mine, closing the small gap. Dark sultry eyes met mine with powerful determination. They smoldered with intensity. His tongue ran across his lips, his hold never wavering. He cupped my cheek gliding his thumb slowly over my skin. Brick and mortar walls stood defenseless against Grady's touch, crashing down into billowing clouds of dust. He pulled me against his strong chest and devoured my lips, holding nothing back.

I matched his urgency in every stroke, feeling every emotion and every touch with passion and need. An explosion of tingles racked my body. Every part of me giving in to melodic rhythm as our bodies swayed together as one compilation of desire. A moan escaped from his soft lips that now lingered below my ear. My head dropped back as kisses trailed around and down my neck, behind my ear and met my swollen lips again.

A throat cleared behind us. "Ten minutes, guys."

Grady grumbled in protest. "Go away, Theo." He rested his forehead against mine; his thumbs slowly traced a path over my jaw. He kissed me again and paused resting his lips against mine. I felt his lips curve up in a smile.

"Charlotte," he whispered. "I've wanted to say that to you for as long as I can remember." Those dark silky eyes captured mine. Somehow, in that moment I knew. Grady had wanted me and only me, and I had serious feelings for this man.

"Kiss me again," I said breathlessly.

He didn't hesitate. He swept me into his arms and took control. My heart pounded against my ribs. There wasn't a bare piece of skin he hadn't kissed or caressed. I wanted to feel every ripple and memorize every piece of him. We poured everything into that kiss knowing it could possibly be the last.

ABOUT THE AUTHOR

A.C. grew up climbing trees and spying on her siblings. When not writing, A.C. can be found cheering on her favorite girls at a softball field, or sitting in her car reading at practices and eating her hidden stash of chocolate. She enjoys family time, traveling, random road trips, watching movies, decorating, and trying new cocktails. She lives in the mitten state with her husband, two daughters, and their furbabies. Terrapin is her first novel.

https://www.goodreads.com/ACTroyer
http://twitter.com/ACTroyer4
www.facebook.com/actroyerfanpage

ACKNOWLEDGEMENTS

I am incredibly grateful to everyone who has helped me turn Terrapin into a real live book.

Endless gratitude to my talented friend, and champion, Trisha Wolfe—how can I ever thank you enough for believing in me? You stuck with me through thick and thin, encouraged me when I needed it the most, and never, never let me give up. To our word-wars, plotting, guidance, the many hour-long conversations, and crazy texts at all hours—I couldn't have done it without you.

"lub u"

To Ryan (Stelle) Mestelle—for your expertise in aviation, answering my millions of questions, and helping me with the correct terminology. I hope I did you proud! Crystal Turner—who has read every draft from Terrapin's inception to publication and never complained, always there to walk me back from the ledge. You're the best original "roomie" any gal could ask for. Donnie Yant for volunteering to be my janitor... You made the cut!

Huge thanks to Andria Cupp, Brandie Metzger, Arlene Sweet, Dana Gregory, Andrea Bell (my jr. beta), Rose Garcia (c.p.), Cara Arver (best neighbor ever), Lani Woodland, Donna Rushton, Mary Edick, Lindsay Mead (my mitten buddy), and Karrie Frederick—for your valuable feedback and comments on the manuscript. Ann (Annibanani) Rought—for our many conversations, writing weekends, and laughs along the way. I'm thankful for our friendship. Melanie Reed—you are the Soul to my Sister, the Carbonation to my Coke, who laughs and cries with me, my hilarious best friend, and the best cheerleader in the hood. Fire up!

To Jim & Jayna Sloan—I'm so lucky to have you in my life. I can't express enough how much your unwavering support and enthusiasm means to me. Thank you for the belly laughs, happy tears, hugs, phone calls and texts. Jayna, you'll always be my "Casper."

Thanks to Sarah at OkayCreations for a cover that blew away my expectations and I'm still in awe of it. Also, to Emily at E.M. Tippetts Book Designs for going above and beyond. You rock!

To my loving parents, Rosemary and DeWayne Gest, for always believing in me, my crazy dreams, and handing down your creative gene. I won the lottery with you. To my siblings, Tarina Jansen, Dennis Gest, and Tom Gest, for invoking my stellar spying skills and hilarious childhood memories. To my in-laws, Deb and Delmar—thank you for believing in me. To my sister-n- law, Christy Lou, I love my coffee cup!

Most of all, thanks to my husband, Jeff, and our girls MaKenzi, and Kamryn—this is for you. I am truly thankful for your patience, listening ears when needed, and encouragement when I wanted to give up. You are my Terrapin, the island that grounds me, my home. Girls, now you can quit asking me when my book will be finished… Mommy did it!

CPSIA information can be obtained at www.ICGtesting.com
Printed in the USA
BVOW05s0948050616

450744BV00004B/138/P